WAR 3: THE LAND OF THE LOU'S   1

EL

WAR

THREE
THE LAND OF THE LOU'S

NATIONAL BESTSELLING AUTHOR

T. STYLES

By T. Styles

ARE YOU ON OUR EMAIL LIST?

SIGN UP ON OUR WEBSITE

www.thecartelpublications.com

OR TEXT THE WORD:

CARTELBOOKS TO 22828

FOR PRIZES, CONTESTS, ETC.

CHECK OUT OTHER TITLES BY THE CARTEL PUBLICATIONS

By *T. Styles*

WWW.THECARTELPUBLICATIONS.COM

WAR 3:

THE LAND OF THE LOU'S

By

T. Styles

PUBLISHER'S NOTE:
This book is a work of fiction. Names, characters,
businesses,
Organizations, places, events and incidents are the
product of the
Author's imagination or are used fictionally. Any
resemblance of
Actual persons, living or dead, events, or locales
are entirely coincidental.

Library of Congress Control Number: 2019933254

ISBN 10: 1948373262

ISBN 13: 978-1948373265

Cover Design: Book Slut Girl

First Edition
Printed in the United States of America

What Up Fam,

I hope this lil' love note finds you all well. It's only February 2019 and already this feels like it's been a very long year. LMAO!

I'm so excited that I have to jump right in to the book in hand! **WAR** MOTHAFUCKIN' **3**! Now I didn't think T could show herself up after the first two installments to this instant classic series, but I sit corrected once again! She tore the pages down! I LOVED LOVED LOVED the backdrop she lays out in this novel to this ongoing "WAR"! Hands down! This one may be my favorite...Don't believe me...Just read! ;)

With that being said, keeping in line with tradition, we want to give respect to a vet or new trailblazer paving the way. In this novel, we would like to recognize:

JORDAN PEELE

Jordan Haworth Peele is an American actor, comedian, writer, producer and director! His

By T. Styles

2017 directorial debut, *"GET OUT"* won him an Academy Award for best original screenplay. His newest release, *"US"* will be out on March 22, 2019 and we will be there to witness his genius front and center. If you are not familiar with his work, get acquainted, he will be around for quite sometime and we at The Cartel Publications are so here for it!

Aight, I've kept you longer than I should have...Goin' and get to it. I'll catch you in the next book.

Be Easy!

Charisse "C. Wash" Washington

Vice President

The Cartel Publications
www.thecartelpublications.com
www.facebook.com/publishercwash
Instagram: publishercwash
www.twitter.com/cartelbooks
www.facebook.com/cartelpublications
Follow us on Instagram: Cartelpublications
#CartelPublications
#UrbanFiction
#PrayForCece
#JordanPeele

#War3

By T. Styles

PROLOGUE
THE PAST

*T*he sun sat on top of the city trying desperately to get the attention of the Baltimore natives below in the midst of project life. But one young man had other ideas in mind for his focus and it wasn't the weather.

Ten-year-old Mason leaned against a squeaky fence in front of the building facing the curb. He was flashy in a way that only a child steeped in dope money could be. A gold chain dripped from his neck. He had a brown paper bag full of snacks at his feet and enough money in his pockets to pay the rent of a desolate individual for two months easily.

To be clear, the young king had not a pressing care in the world.

In the moment anyway.

He and his friend Tangelo were watching three girls about their age switch friskily in front of them as they recited cheers. They smelled of sweat and corn chips but Mason didn't care what scent they brought with them from their musty homes. They were promiscuous in their youth and as a result,

Mason didn't mind dry humping them in the Laundromat of his building, while playing Hide-N-Go Get It if they gave him the nod.

The young girls had just kicked the show up another notch by shaking their undeveloped hips harder, when the building's door opened. Curious about who was coming out to play, Mason turned around to see who was stepping onto the stage.

And boy did he get a show.

Walking out of the building was the prettiest girl he'd ever seen in his young life. His official crush. Everything she did appeared to be done with grace, even sitting on the step while holding a stack of composition books and pencils. Of course he'd seen her before.

But always in passing.

She moved into their building with her mother and father just last week. He even saw her in school and a few times walking into the building but she never said a word.

Not to boys or other girls.

She was mysterious.

Her skin, the color of vanilla.

Her scent, that of fresh apples.

She was a vision and even soaked in adolescence, Mason knew enough to realize that

By T. Styles

she was different. Untouched by the streets of Baltimore, mainly because she avoided it all.

Even the young girls, who jealously watched Mason's attention from them drift off, couldn't help but stamp her beauty. They answered to his disconnect by winding their bodies faster, and harder, hoping to regain the son of a drug dealer's awareness.

It didn't work.

This was the first time his crush had paused and Mason was fascinated as he watched her write vigorously in a composition book. He needed to get closer.

Just a little. He was simply too far to see her silky long hair, which extended down her back, playfully caress her cheeks in the warm breeze.

And so he bopped over in her direction.

Carefully.

As if each step mattered.

Maybe they did.

"Want me to come?" Tangelo yelled out to his friend.

Mason ignored him as his answer. Not bothering to even look the boy's way.

Tangelo responded by digging into his snack bag, something that would've gotten him dropped kicked if Mason wasn't distracted.

Sitting on the step next to the girl, he looked at her face closely. Although her fingertips moved while holding the pencil, the rest of her body was as still as a mannequin. In her perceived spurn, he could observe every feature clearly.

He was taken aback at how although he sat within inches of her, she didn't appear to notice he was alive. She was in a world of her own. All of her attention was on the sketch of an island that was coming into view before his eyes.

"H...hi," he stuttered. "What you...I mean...that's nice." He pointed at the book.

Slowly her eyes moved and for the first time, she was looking directly at him, and he felt weak in the knees. At ten-years-old her gaze said she was wise beyond her years and had already dealt with more pain than someone twenty years her senior.

And still she smiled.

"My name's Mason," he continued. "Mason Louisville." He swallowed the lump in his throat, even though another felt as if it had taken its place.

She put her pencil down and extended her tiny hand. "I'm Blakeslee Wales." Her hair blew in her face and she tucked it behind her ear. "It's nice to meet you, Mason."

CHAPTER ONE
MONTHS EARLIER
FRIDAY NIGHT

A dark, cloudless purple sky. Golden specks in clear view. It was all so miraculous.

But as Banks sat on the beach of Wales Island, overlooking the ocean, with stars so brilliant they could've blinded him, he could've been looking at shit in a toilet bowl and his feelings would've been the same.

The man was in extreme despair.

His daughter was missing. His son, Harris was in prison and if he was being honest, he hadn't fully come to terms with losing Mason Louisville, his best friend, by his own hands. He was certain that being on an island he envisioned as a child would help soothe his depression. But nothing worked.

He just couldn't get right.

As the water lapped at his feet, he took a deep breath and called Rev, his best soldier back in his hometown. He was hoping that he would have good news, no matter how trivial but that's not what happened.

By T. Styles

"The line is secure right?" Banks asked.

"Always." He paused. "And I'm sorry, Banks, but we still don't have any news." He paused. "We haven't stopped looking since you left but we can't find her anywhere. I know this isn't what you wanted to hear."

Banks sighed.

"Are you sure they checked the outer acres of the property? Before I blew up Mason's crib, I saw Minnie run into the woods." He shifted a little on the sand. "Listen, Rev...I have a feeling she's alive out there somewhere. And I...I..." He took a deep breath. "...You have to find my daughter. I can't accept anything less."

He may have been hard on Rev at times, but Rev made himself available for Banks this way. Having met Banks through his father when he was alive, it was as if Rev was sent to protect him.

"I understand and we really have searched hard. I personally oversaw the operation. But there was no sign of her, sir." He paused. "We would've still been out there but the police came by checking the ruins from the bomb that was detonated. I'll have to fall back at least until Monday."

Frustrated, Banks grabbed the beer can that sat nestled in the sand at his feet and wiped his hand down his face. "What about Harris?" He took a huge gulp. "Anything on him yet?"

"Right now everything is going as planned," he paused. "We gonna put the move on Linden the moment we can."

"I don't trust that he won't try us first." He paused. "So stay up on your connections in the prison. If they get any idea that something's off, I need us to hit him hard."

"Banks." When he turned around he saw Bet walking toward him. She was wearing a shimmering see-through swimsuit cover up, and a black one-piece bathing suit. "Are you okay? I've been looking for you everywhere. Why are you out here alone?"

He faced forward. "I'll call you back, Rev. Whatever you do, don't stop searching. My heart is still beating. That means she's still alive."

"Sure thing, boss."

With the phone at his side, he took a deep breath. "I just wanted to get some fresh air." He hated that she always seemed to crowd his space when he wanted to be alone. She made things as awkward between them as three titties.

18   *By T. Styles*

She sat next to him and leaned her head against his shoulder. "Heard anything about the kids? I keep having the most confused dreams and I...I guess I'm trying to be strong. It's just so hard with us being here you know?"

"I haven't heard anything yet." He drank all of his beer and crushed the can...it crackled.

She looked over at him. Her stare was intense, almost as if she didn't believe him. "We are a team, Banks."

Silence.

"And I know you think I can't handle what's going on but you couldn't be more wrong." She continued. "You just have to—"

"What do you want?" He glared.

She looked down. "Dinner is almost ready."

He nodded. "Good. Go eat."

"Not without you." She touched his hand. "It smells delicious too," she continued. "The Nunez family does such a nice job taking—"

"What do you *really* want, Bet?" He burped, and wiped his mouth with the back of his hand. "I know you. Whatever is really on your mind come out and say it. Instead of doing your best to irritate me with small talk."

She stroked his growing beard, which hadn't been shaped up since they'd been on Wales Island. "Do you love me anymore?" Her hand dropped. "Do you even love our family?"

He shook his head.

"What, Banks? Stop using silence as a way to punish me when you know I can't handle it."

"I'm not walking through that door with you. Pick a fight with a rock or something."

She rolled her eyes. "Are you angry about our kids or Mason?" She threw her hands up in the air. "Can you at least tell me that?"

He rotated his head quickly in her direction. "Why you keep that nigga's name on your tongue?"

"I know you miss him, Banks," she paused. "My only question is do you miss him more than you miss Minnie? Or Harris?"

"I'm not answering stupid questions. And if you must know, I placed moves in motion to get Harris out of that prison. Soon as I get the word that it's carried through, I'll be on my way."

She shook her head, stood up and looked down at him. The warm breeze caressed her body, allowing her shawl to float behind her like wings. "I have been more patient with you than—"

"Fuck else do you want me to say?" He yelled looking up at her. "Huh? That I blame myself for Minnie being lost? Or that it's my fault that Harris is in jail because I was trying to get a plane instead of taking you all out of Baltimore when I had the chance? Fuck do you want from me?"

She trembled as tears rolled down her face. Taking a deep breath she wiped them away and looked at the ocean. Hoping it would calm her agitated spirit. "You are the wealthiest man I have ever known. Could even afford your own world. And all you did was bring your ugly insecurities from Baltimore to a beautiful place."

He shook his head. "What does that mean?"

"You gotta deal with your own shit, Banks. If you don't like who you are, moving here won't change it. All you going to do is put us in hell with you."

"I'm five minutes from laying hands on you."

"Do it! I'm begging you! If you did, at least I would know you're alive!" She took a deep breath. "I'm not feeling like myself, Banks. And I don't know if I want this anymore. I don't know if I want us anymore. But I already know you don't care." She walked away.

When she was gone Banks took a deep breath. Everything with Bet was heavy. Ordinarily he would have his coke business and kids as an escape back home. But being alone on the island with her made him weary.

He needed relief.

"I don't know what to do anymore," Banks said to himself. "I don't know what to do about anything...about..." Banks' head hung as he looked at the sand under his feet. "Why am I even here?"

Who was he speaking to?

He didn't know.

But not too far from where he sat stood a small wooden shed used to keep their towels and lawn chairs. But in the moment this space also held Mason, who was hidden from view but within earshot of it all. He had been looking through the slats of the structure.

"I feel you, man," he whispered to himself. "We two niggas from Baltimore in the middle of nowhere."

By **T.** *Styles*

Holding a Glencairn whisky glass against his lips, Banks strolled down the spacious luxurious hallway of his mansion. The white linen short sleeve shirt he wore was slightly open; showcasing his muscles and the large tattoo of raven wings that covered the surgery scars he had at eighteen, to remove his breasts.

Still, he knew he was king.

Inebriated, his steps were a little rocky as he moved but his swagger allowed him to stay on his feet.

This dining room was spectacular.

The automatic ceiling was open and showcased the brilliant stars above the silver and gold dining room tablecloth that hosted an array of Spanish cuisine meals. There was lamb, fish, rice, potatoes and vegetables. And along the center of the table were four gold candelabras, which flickered with fire.

Bet was on the opposite end of the table, Spacey was on the left and Joey was on the right. They were also dressed in white and the moonlight from above along with the glow from the candlelight made their skin glimmer.

Placing his glass down, Banks took his position at the head of the table.

For a moment he thought about how things used to be, when the Lou's joined them for dinner. But now, despite being amongst so much beauty, he felt further away from his family. He felt further away from himself. And when he looked into his wife's eyes, even from a far, he could feel their disconnection widening.

Rosa, the matriarch of the Nunez family, walked up to Banks and refreshed his whiskey glass. Her grey and black hair was brushed up into a neat ballerina bun. Her features said she was innocent but her presence spoke of darker times that not even Banks was aware of. Even her smile was fixed...like a picture on a wall.

The agreement, between the Wales' and the Nunez family although respectful, was serious. Banks required that each of them care for his family and handle all chores, and in return he would give them a modest salary and a place to stay for the rest of their lives. Both families he was certain would grow in size and with Banks as the anchor, they would create an island of people who would love and respect each other for who they were, and not their pasts.

He forgot one part.

In order to build a better future, you must acknowledge and understand the history.

"Thank you," Banks said to Rosa. "Everything looks beautiful tonight."

"My pleasure, sir," she looked at him and then the other Wales members. "Would you like anything else?" As with other members of her family, her Hispanic accent was thick and full of culture.

"We're fine." Bet grabbed a wine bottle from the ice bucket on the table. Mounds of crushed ice fell into the bosom of her breasts as she poured the burgundy liquid down her gullet. Red lines wiggled down the sides of her face before stopping at the center of her ear.

He was disgusted.

She was a mess.

"Uh, yes," Banks said looking up at Rosa, holding her fragile wrist aggressively. Also drunk, he wasn't as smooth as he was in the past. "Why don't you and your family join us for dinner tonight?"

Her eyes widened with surprise and delight at the same time. Since they'd all been on the island together, it was as if he was doing his best to keep the families separate. The poor versus the rich. The powerful vs. the weak. The Wales' vs. The Nunez's.

So what brought about the change?

"Are you...are you sure, sir?"

He nodded.

"Thank you, sir. I'll get my family right away," she placed the whiskey bottle on the table and tiptoed with expediency out of the room, as if worried he would change his mind.

Within two minutes the Nunez family was present.

The first to enter was Rosa's husband, Ives. Shorter in stature than his 5'7" wife, he was a bundled mess of a man who always seemed on edge. Behind him came twenty-eight-year-old Tobias, a workhorse by nature, he was cold. A handsome young man who screamed confidence and sex appeal. In America he would be an extreme catch knocking many women out of their Ugg boots.

Next was twenty-one-year-old Cassandra and nineteen-year-old Emetine who was so beautiful; to insecure women their looks would be considered offensive. Their thick black luxurious hair dripped over their shoulders and they exuded sex in more ways than one. Through their

By T. *Styles*

eyes, the way they moved and even the things that they said. These Spanish mami's were bred to seduce.

Then there was fifteen-year-old Roxana who Banks assumed was mute because she never spoke. Still, she was far from dumb. The little girl, although quiet, saw it all.

Finally there was twenty-two-year-old Oswalda. Weighing in at over 250 pounds for her 5'5" frame, she was a big girl but it didn't block her beauty. She was fully aware how to work the curves of her body, and as a result her boobs and ass were initially the first things you saw when she entered the room. But it was her eyes that gave her intentions away. Most of the time to her disadvantage.

As Emetine sat closely to Spacey and Cassandra sat next to Joey, since they had already been acquainted, the rest of the Nunez family found available seats around the luxurious table.

When everyone was in position, Banks smiled and just like that, his table was filled with bodies, the way he preferred it.

Raising his glass, he stood up and looked around at the blended people. "From here on out, this is how I want it to be. The Wales and the Nunez family together, on this beautiful island, making a life for ourselves."

He took a sip and seat.

Cassandra gripped Joey's hand in excitement of the news. To be in the company of kings was a beautiful thing.

Emetine kissed Spacey on the cheek.

And Oswalda glared at her siblings.

But it was Bet who made quite a spectacle, by laughing loudly.

He glared at her from across the table. "Fuck so funny?"

"You funny, nigga," she said as spit mixed with wine flew from her lips. "Always using people as pawns. Placing...placing people in position for your games. What is it, Banks Wales? Do you hate yourself so much that you need faces around you to prevent you from seeing your own?"

His jaw twitched.

"I...I don't care what you do," Bet continued, standing up before meeting her seat again quickly with a loud thud. Her ass cheeks stung a little but she was too drunk to stop while she was

By T. Styles

ahead. "You ain't gonna find peace until you deal with your own shit, *boss.*" She giggled.

"Bet, I'm warning you."

She stood up again and Spacey quickly moved toward his mother. But she stopped him with a palm in his direction. "I'm fine, son. I been standing...standing on my...own since...we got to this dreaded place and I'll stand on my own now."

"Ma, sit down," Joey begged. "*Please.*"

She planted one hand on the table and the other on the wine bottle. Her dress fought desperately to shield her nakedness but it was struggling. Slithering down her shoulder like a snake.

"I will not, because I know...I know what he doing," she pointed at Banks with the spout of the bottle. "And no matter how...how hard you try, Banks Wales," she burped, "You can't replace my son and daughter. And you can't replace the Lou's. Your *precious fucking Lou's*, that you always loved more than you did your own people."

"Sit the fuck down, Bet," he said through clenched teeth.

"No!" She yelled. "You sit down." She stumbled again and just like that, the boys saw their mother's breasts for the first time since they were babies.

And with God's grace, both prayed they'd never see them again.

Always on duty, Oswalda quickly stood up and helped Bet reclaim her honor, by shielding her breasts with her bare palms. "Come with me, Mrs. Wales." She said holding her firmly against her plush body. "Don't you worry about one thing. I have you."

Banks was vexed at his wife's crass behavior.

It had only been a matter of days and it appeared that overnight Bet had begun to unravel before his very own eyes.

He understood why she was upset.

Of course he did!

He was hurt that their kids weren't with them too. But it wasn't like he didn't have people scouring the wreckage of the Lou Estate for Minnie. And it wasn't like he didn't hire pariah in the prison that held Harris, to be sure they would be reunited soon and that he would remain safe. He hated her for not being patient and her weakness made him question making her his wife.

After she made her sloppy exit, he flopped in his seat and drank what was left of the whisky. Every eye was upon him, each secretly wondering if the man, who was considered their king, could bring things under control.

"All is well," he assured them, pouring a little more into his cup. Smiling widely than he normally had in the past, he took a deep breath. "Now...let us eat!"

CHAPTER TWO

The ocean was tranquil as it lapped the beach.

Mason was in a peaceful sleep on a bed of towels in the back of the shed, for a moment without a care in the world. Where he was positioned, even if someone walked inside, they would have no reason to go all the way to the back. So he was tucked away just right. However if they went too far, their brains would be splattered behind them because he had no intention on being caught.

When he heard someone walk inside, he grabbed his gun within reach and aimed. With eyes on who was present, he wiped a hand down his face, placed the gun down and sighed.

It was Oswalda.

Standing in front of him holding a plate of food, she grinned. There was something she wanted from him, although she had yet to express it fully within their brief time of getting to know one another. However, outsiders looking in would believe her motives to be sexual. Having changed up for the evening, she was now wearing

By T. Styles

a pink chiffon dress that showed the soft folds of her skin but more importantly her thick breasts.

"You look so peaceful," she said, with her heavy accent. "I wish I could be as free as you."

He smiled and shook his head. "Your big pretty ass scared the fuck outta me. Luckily for you I didn't squeeze."

She closed the door and handed him the warm plate of food. Sitting in front of him yoga style, her flower opened just enough so he could see her intentions if he craved a little pussy with dinner.

Sitting up straight, he dug into the meal with his fingers, scooping first rice, followed by meat. "I see what you doing." He chewed heavily. "But I ain't buying."

She smiled and closed her thighs a little upon hearing the rejection. "I ain't selling."

He looked at her open tunnel. "Sure 'bout that?" He shoveled more food into his mouth.

She sighed. "Tell me again. About America."

He shrugged and folded a slab of lamb into his mouth. The man wanted to eat. Not speak on tales of dope, hustlers and the women who loved them. "What you wanna know?"

"Everything."

He shook his head. "I keep telling you that the best in life is right here," his mouth was full of food. "On the beach you have peace. The air is fresh and you can always—"

"Why am I helping you again?" She glared. "You won't humor me. You won't tell me who you really are. Just what exactly am I getting out of this relationship?"

He smiled and continued to eat. "Maybe you should make clear what you're after. Start there. Because the way you acting, you look desperate." His brash way of speaking to her brought her great discomfort.

"I'm not desperate," she spat. "I'm helping because I caught you in here, without the boss knowing and you needed help. And you promised me you would tell me about America if I brought you food and—"

"I'm not your hero," he said putting his plate down while brushing his hands together. "If you looking for that you—"

Suddenly, she stood on her knees and slapped him. "Then you lied!" She said pointing in his face. "You fucking lied and I can't stand liars, mister!"

The tension in the shed grew thick.

34   *By* *T. Styles*

Mason's nostrils opened and pulsated as he shot daggers her way. Slowly he rose and she did the same. The moment they were on their feet, toe to toe, he stole her in the mouth as if he were Floyd Mayweather. Helping her up by her dress, he stole her again.

"You act like a spoiled princess instead of a maid," Mason eyed her closer. "Who are you?"

"I hate you!"

He chuckled. "Like I said before...American niggas ain't no place for you to keep your dreams."

As her lip swole before his eyes, she moved toward the door. "I wonder what Banks will say if he finds out you here." She cried, blood pouring down her mouth and onto her pink chiffon dress. "I don't know who you are, but if you hiding I know he don't want you here."

He smiled, sat back down and grabbed his plate. "Do what you feel the need to do. But start with getting the fuck up out my face."

Tucked in a small house in Landover, Maryland, Jersey was cleaning dishes after the huge meal she prepared for Dragon, Derrick, Patterson and Howard. Most of her family was present, with the exception of her husband but she was very worried. Mainly because Arlyndo wasn't home, and all she could do was pray that he was fine.

After she put the final dish on the rack, Dragon walked up behind her and placed his hands on her waist, before kissing her softly on the side of her chin. She quickly turned around and looked up at his vanilla colored face.

"What are you doing?" She whispered, looking around him, and into the living room where her sons sat watching TV. Luckily none of them appeared to see the disrespectful move. "You can't do this...especially not in front of my children."

"Men..." he said. "They're men, start treating them that way." He paused. "Besides, I'm not doing anything. Except saying thank you for the meal."

"Well don't touch me like that," she said firmly. "Ever."

He took one step back and shook his head. He was agitated but he was trying desperately to place his bully back in the cage, where it couldn't hurt anyone. "You gonna help me?"

"Now?"

He walked away.

Wiping her hand on the dishtowel, she placed both palms on the sink and took a deep breath. All of her life she found herself in the company of men who took more than they were willing to put back in her life, and Dragon was no different.

"Help me, God," she whispered. "I don't know if I have the strength to go through this again."

Tossing the dishtowel on the sink, she walked into the bedroom. Derrick, who was wearing a bandage over his amputated toe, watched as she disappeared from sight.

As Dragon sat on the edge of the bed, Jersey walked to the closet and removed a set of blue slacks. She placed them on the mattress, dropped to her knees and helped him remove his jeans. Next, with him looking down at her, she placed each of his legs into the pants.

Just like when they were kids, he seemed unable to do the simplest of chores on his own, whenever she was near. For a moment she wondered how he got along without her in the years gone by and then he remembered seeing the name Megan on his cell phone when they were sleep in bed.

Did she do all of the things he wanted, too?

When he stood up, she walked to the closet and grabbed his blue police uniform shirt and placed it on him, brushing invisible dust off his shoulders. As he zippered his pants and buttoned his shirt, she grabbed his gun belt and slipped it around his waist. All while he smiled at her, with extreme satisfaction.

"I'm happy you're here," he said. "And I know you don't like to talk much about whatever this is between us, but it's important for you to know how I feel. I never got to do that before when we were together and it was my biggest regret."

"Is that your *only* regret?" She grabbed a brush and stroked his brown hair into submission. "Because I have many."

His eyes were penetrating and she wondered if he heard anything she said. "It feels like it did back in the day when—"

"This is temporary," she said looking up at him, directly into his eyes. Something she never

By T. Styles

would've done back in the day. "This isn't my home. You understand this don't you?"

"I know," his smile was as tight as a stretched rubber band, ready to pop on her ass. "I just need you to realize that you can stay with me as long as you want. With me you will always have a home and you will always be safe. Without me I can't guarantee your safety or your sanity."

That was a threat.

And she heard it loud and clear.

"I know you're protecting me, Dragon, but I..." she looked down. "I...I can't stay here. You keep saying you understand but your words...how you treat me in front of my children, tells me you feel differently. I'm a married woman. You must remember that. We talked about this all before. Me and my sons are here just until—"

"Men!" He snapped. "Why can't you call them who they are? You put everything on the line for them, as if they're still children. You weaken them that way, Jersey."

She blinked. "I will always look at them like boys. I will always treat them like they are my babies, in a way I wished someone did for me when I was a kid."

"They're men," he repeated, wanting to shoot each of them, so that he'd never have to talk about them again. "Not boys and not children."

She nodded. There was no use in talking to him. He had his opinion, which he would protect at all cost. And she held hers. For the moment it was best to leave the matter alone.

He wiped her hair back and kissed her forehead. "Thank you," he frowned as he walked into the bathroom.

When the door was closed, he locked it and stomped toward the mirror. Opening it, he removed the backing from the lowest wall in the cabinet. Placing it on the sink, he withdrew a revolver out of a secret compartment. With the weapon in his hand, he sat on the edge of the tub. As slowly as possible, his finger moved over the trigger and he swallowed the lump in his throat. With his index finger over the trigger, he pressed it down and...

CLICK!

Opening the chamber, it was empty.

As if relieved, he stood up, placed the gun and it's paneling back in the secret chamber and closed the mirror. Taking a look at his flushed face, he wiped a hand back over his brown hair.

By T. Styles

Dragon was attractive, and his looks are what brought many women to their end.

Some mentally.

Others by way of a slow death.

Grinning at himself, he took a deep breath and walked out of the room and past Jersey who had been sitting on the bed. His smile said he was fine but his disposition said rage.

"Did you want me to make you breakfast in the—"

SLAM!

Dragon closed the door cutting off her sentence and stormed out the front door.

Jersey wiped her hand down her face just as Derrick strolled inside using his wheelchair. The moment she saw his face, she smiled and took a deep breath. Trying to put on that all was well.

"Hey, honey, do you want more food? I can warm—"

"Ma, I don't like him. I told you that before, and I know you tired of me saying it, but he's trouble. He's trouble for us all."

She nodded and suppressed the urge to cry. "I know..."

"So why we here?" He rolled closer.

"Derrick, just—"

WAR 3: THE LAND OF THE LOU'S 41

When her cell phone rang she ran over to the dresser and picked it up. Looking at the screen she felt an immediate sense of relief. "It's your father. Let me talk to him in private. And no matter what, keep what's going on with Dragon away from Mason. I don't want him to worry."

He nodded, moved toward the door and closed it behind himself.

She took a deep breath. "Mason, where are you?"

"Whoa, I thought you were still mad at me. Haven't spoken to you since the first time I got here. To be honest I ain't even think you would answer the phone. Decided to try anyway. Glad I did."

"The boys were keeping me up on what was happening with you," she said. "But Mason, I need to know...I need..." she sobbed quietly.

"Jersey, what is it? Why you crying?"

"I messed up," she said softly. "I messed up and I think...I mean...I think I put us in more trouble than we need right now."

"Is somebody hurting you?" He asked firmly.

"No...I mean—"

By *T. Styles*

"Where's your brother?" He paused. "Let him know what's going on until I get back. You said he got you right?"

Her heart thumped in her chest.

He was the problem and yet she couldn't say a mumbling word.

"Jersey, did you tell your brother what's going on or not? Since I feel like you don't wanna tell me."

"I just want to get out of here," Jersey said. "I want to get out of here now, Mason. And I don't care where we go or what we do, as long as we're together, as a family."

"Trust me, I got a place. I just need some time to sort things out."

She fell back on the bed and looked straight up at the ceiling. "When will I see you?"

"Hopefully in a matter of days," he paused. "Just hang in there."

"Hurry, Mason. Please hurry."

CHAPTER THREE

Oswalda had just finished icing her face when her mother walked into the kitchen. The moment she saw her she stumbled backwards in shock. "What happened to you?" She rushed up to her and dragged a dry thumb over her swollen mouth. "Who hit you?" She was speaking in their native language, as they always did when they were alone.

Oswalda slapped her hand away. "As if you care," she glared. "Because lets be real *mother*, you never really want to know what's happening with me."

Rosa stepped back. "Why is it that you, that you hate so deeply? We may not have the best now but we—"

"I hate what's happening here," Oswalda corrected her. "I have a hard life."

"Oswalda, your hard life is not my fault. If anything I tried to shield you from it all. I tried to help you. Why don't you just enjoy what's happening now and refrain from bringing up the past?"

"Mother, we are slaves!"

By T. Styles

"We aren't slaves," Rosa glared. "I have been enslaved in my lifetime. I have been forced to kill innocent people, because that's what the militia wanted. You never had those worries. Trust me, there is a difference."

"I thought, I thought they said they would make us their wives."

Rosa looked behind herself and then back at her daughter. "Oswalda, be patient. Why can't you ever be patient?" She threw her hands up. "Everything with you has to be right now and some day you'll find yourself at the mercy of your anxiousness. If you aren't careful, you're going to say or do the wrong thing that will get you hurt, and I don't want that to happen."

"You haven't answered my question, mother!" She yelled. "I like Spacey and he...he doesn't even know I'm alive. What is wrong with me?" She looked down at her t-shirt and jeans. "Why aren't I pretty enough?"

"Give things time and we won't have to deal with these matters anymore. That's all I can say right now."

"Time for what? For Emetine or Cassandra to take them both away? Why am I the only one who is made to feel so...so..." she looked down at her body and cried. "I hate myself."

Rosa walked up to her and held her tightly. Separating from her, she placed her face between her palms and looked into her eyes. "You're beautiful, Oswalda."

She sniffled and then looked down at herself. In her mind mounds of flesh upon flesh couldn't be considered beautiful. "Fuck you," she said. "I don't need anybody. You hear me? I don't need anybody but myself!"

In rage she stormed away. She had just passed the bowling alley where Spacey, Emetine Joey and Cassandra, were playing inside. She paused in envy. Their happiness sent chills up her spine and had her thinking wild thoughts. She decided to double back and break up the party.

"Are you going to help me clean up or not?" Oswalda yelled, standing at the entrance, fists stabbed into her hips.

Her sisters turned around and looked at her.

In that moment, all laughter ceased.

"What happened to your face?" Spacey asked, as if truly concerned.

"Nothing, sir," she said under her breath. She wanted to go off on him but she couldn't bring herself to disrespect the boss. Despite hating that she desired him. Focusing on her sisters she said, "Come on, now. You have to help me clean the—"

"Get outta here," Joey said waving his hand at her. "We not trying to hear all that shit you popping. Whatever need be done can wait. And if it can't do it yourself."

Oswalda was stunned. "But we..."

"Get the fuck out!" Joey yelled again, pointing at her. "Don't make me tell you again."

"Yes...yes, sir." Embarrassed above all else, Oswalda turned around and stormed out, bare feet slapping against the marble floor. To make her shame worse, the moment she walked down the hall, she could hear their laughter again. The sounds of their voices enraged her and had her considering murder.

But she would figure out how to get revenge on them in another way, especially Joey.

She just had to be more creative.

The running shower made the air thick.

Banks ran his hand down his face and walked closer to the water, allowing the beating drops to soothe him. There were a lot of questions on his mind. Most of them were wrapped up in forms of the word *why*.

Why hadn't things gotten better now that they were on Wales Island? Although the boys had settled in, Bet seemed to be worsening by the hour. Why hadn't they found Minnie? Why did he worry so much about Harris and why did Mason's murder fuck with his head the way it had? Although he would never admit it aloud, he wondered if it was better to have an enemy he loved alive instead of dead?

Taking the washcloth and soap, he worked the rag to a rich white foam. First he washed his face while dragging the cloth down his neck and across his chest. Then he washed his arms, back and legs followed closely after.

Next he washed his rear and rinsed again.

The next portion of his bathing routine always weighed heavily on him, often leaving him emotionally drained. So, before doing anything else, he grabbed the glass of whiskey that sat on

By T. Styles

a table outside of the shower. It had become such a ritual that he never stopped to reflect why he needed to have a drink for this part of his hygiene routine. It was simply the way things had always been.

Had he stopped to do a little self-reflection, just a little, the answer on why he needed liquor would be made clear. It was because in the shower, with his clothes off, was the only time he would be forced to face what he chose to ignore all of his life.

That he was a woman.

With a vagina.

That he despised.

After drinking all of the liquor, allowing the warmth to run down his throat, he took a deep breath. Then he rinsed his washcloth and drowned it with soap. Next he wrapped the cloth around the tips of his fingers, so that he wouldn't have to touch himself. So that he could disconnect from the opening of his body that hadn't been touched since he and Mason had sex. And so he wiped himself thoroughly but as quickly as possible, hoping the terrible moment would be over sooner than later.

He had just finished when the door flew open.

Banks was stunned because everyone knew, even prior to being made aware that he was female, that walking in on him in such a private place would lead to him lashing out violently.

So who was there?

"I'm in here!" He yelled.

"Banks," Bet said softly. "I just wanna...I mean...I know you're angry with me."

"Bet, what you doing?" His jaw clicked. "I'll talk to you after I'm—"

She closed the bathroom door and walked further inside.

"I know, I know you want your privacy." She moved closer to the shower door. "But I'm better now. I think I finally get what you want from me and I'll try my best to...to not make you so angry with me all of the time."

If she truly meant her words she was doing a bad job.

His nostrils flared as he watched the silhouette of her frame through the stained glass.

Don't come in here. He thought.

"And I know you think I'm losing my mind but..." She yanked the door open and entered. "...just try not to be so mad."

He was so angry he felt faint.

By T. Styles

Never.

Ever!

Had they shared a shower together with him being naked. One night when they had a lot to drink he visited her while she was bathing and sucked her pussy dry but that was the extent of his madness. In fact, he was wearing a white T and grey sweatpants that showed the imprint of his dildo even on that day. This was a major infringement on their agreement as a couple and yet she was too out of her mind, too silly in her thoughts, to realize the infraction.

The bottom line was simple.

Bet was violating in the worst way. And at best putting their marriage in extreme jeopardy. But instead of sensing his rage, she eased behind him and wrapped her arms around his waist. Her dangling fingertips were inches from his...well... *pussy*.

Had she touched it he would've killed her.

"Don't be mad at me anymore, Banks. All I want is a truce. All I want is peace."

He was frozen with fear that she might touch him, and maybe even look at him differently. In his mind she had no idea that he was actually female. He had somewhat bought into his own delusion.

From the waist up he was created like he wanted others to see him. With his beard, chiseled chest and tattooed torso. But below...nothing had changed because there was no surgeries existing, which would guarantee a penis, would remain intact.

"Bet..." his breath mixed with whiskey and rage floated along the steam. "...you must want me to hate you, forever."

Hearing his words, she backed up into the wall and flopped on the shower bench. The water drenched her body.

Once she released him, he jumped out, grabbed his towel and quickly slid on his soft black sweats and white beater. Once dressed, walking back up to the shower he fought with what to say. Part of him wanted to unleash but as he looked into her eyes he could tell something was wrong.

Why couldn't she be the best version of herself, when she knew what he was dealing with?

That quickly he was taken back to the many moments he and his father, Dennis, had to hold

52   *By T. Styles*

his mother down because her bipolar episodes had flared up so badly she could hurt herself and others.

One day in particular he remembered when his father and mother were taking him to Kings Dominion. Banks was the most excited he had ever been. As he sat in the passenger seat and looked over at his father, he was filled with love, despite the issues he was dealing with about them doing all they could to make him appear feminine on that day. Even down to the yellow dress and long soft ponytails running down his back.

Still, that day started out almost perfect. He relented to allowing them to dress him up and his mother even allowed him to ride in the front so he could sightsee during the trip. And then, just that quickly, things changed.

They were in standstill traffic leading into the park, when all of a sudden they turned around, only to see his mother completely naked. Banks was so enthralled by his surroundings and going to the amusement park that he couldn't recall when she found the time to disrobe. As if that wasn't enough, to make matters worse she bolted from the car and ran into traffic, her pale white skin flushed with excitement. It took his father and two male strangers to bring her back to safety as he sat in the front seat, tears dropping on his yellow dress.

Needless to say Kings Dominion was cancelled.

And still he loved his mother.

Despite her leaving him alone for many days after Dennis was arrested. One episode even resulting in her getting pregnant by a stranger. He had been through it all with Angie. But for some reason he didn't have one ounce of sympathy for Bet, who was obviously going through the same mental issues.

"You hate me," she sniffled. "I can tell the way you look at me that you hate..." she smiled, although her heart broke inside. "...you hate me because I'm not her...tell the truth, Banks. You'll feel better when you do. I promise."

CHAPTER FOUR

Banks sat in his parlor drinking warm whiskey that Rosa prepared for him next to the heatless fireplace. He needed the treat because he was speaking to Harris on the phone, which always caused him great distress. One of his children being locked up and him not being able to help was unbearable.

And yet he was forced to do just that.

"Listen, I'm getting you out of that place." He paused. "I don't want you worrying because—"

"Niggas in here wanna kill me, Pops." His breath was heavy. "They trying to intimidate me and—"

"CALM DOWN!" Banks yelled slamming his drink on the table. A few droplets splattered out. "Look where you are." He paused. "You really want to be seen as weak right now? I need you to pull yourself together."

Harris breathed heavily. "I'm sorry, I just, I just ain't think it was gonna be like this," he said softly.

"Listen, I can't say much so let me say this...my reach is long and you will be safe. In the mean time go by your middle name. Don't tell people who you are and more than anything don't allow fear to be seen from your eyes. They want you to break down."

"What if something goes wrong, Pops?"

Banks sat back and sighed. He sounded like his mother. "You been listening to Bet again?"

"No, but I—"

"Well I said I got you. At this point in the game I really need you to start trusting me."

"But what if you miss something?"

Banks' jaw twitched.

"Pops, you there?"

"Nothing will happen to you." He grabbed his drink and took a sip. "I put that on my life." He wiped his lips and sat back as Oswalda strolled into the lounge.

"Okay, Pops...I gotta go."

"Son!" Banks yelled, wanting to get something off his heart. He needed him to know how he felt and at the same time, saying the words right now felt wrong.

"Yes?"

Banks looked at Oswalda and focused back on the call, "Nothing...I'll see you soon."

"See you soon."

When the call was done he placed his phone down on the sofa and focused on her. He never really acknowledged her because her energy always put him off. But she was a Nunez, and since the families had an agreement, he had to take her for what she was worth.

Still, she was dressed inappropriately, the soft folds of her flesh visible with the slightest glance. If he could say anything about her, it was that she changed clothes more than a superstar at a concert. "What happened to your face?" He drank the rest of his whiskey and sat the glass down, before crossing his legs, his ankle on his knee.

She touched her lip. "Oh...nothing." She smiled. "I...I was messing around and hurt myself. Nobody's fault but my own." She cleared her throat. "Uh, sir, can I get you anything?"

"No." He looked at his dry glass. "On second thought, warm me up another." He raised his glass.

"Of course." She removed it from his hand and turned to leave. When she made it to the door, she turned back around. "Sir, may I tell you something?"

Silence.

His lack of response had her questioning if she was making the best move. But still she continued anyway. "I just wanted to say..." she cleared her throat. "...My sisters were bowling and not helping me with the chores tonight. I know you like a clean home and—"

He glared and leaned in, his elbows on his knees, fingers clasped together. "Do I look like the lady of the house?"

Her eyebrows rose. "No but—"

"Then don't ever come at me with some small shit like that again. I'm paying you and your family to do a job. The day you give me the impression you can't handle it will be the day you gotta get the fuck up out my house."

"Sure...I...I understand." She turned around and exited quickly.

Feeling dumber than a bag of left shoes, on the way out, she ran into Spacey in the hallway. He was holding flowers but was wearing a frown. She looked down at them and smiled, her heart skipped several beats just being close to him. "Hi." She waved. "I was just—"

"Why you do that?"

She swallowed. "Do what?"

"Go to my father about my brother? And your sisters?"

She moved uneasily on her feet. His eyes said he disapproved but she didn't know why. "Because they weren't helping and I want things to be nice for you and your family. I figured—"

"The fucked up part is, you were gonna be my reason." He pointed at her face.

She was thrown off. "Your reason for what?"

"It doesn't matter anymore." He dropped the flowers and walked away.

Confused, she bent down to pick them up and a piece of paper was tucked securely within the pedals. She unfolded the note. It read:

O, you look prettier when you smile.

She dropped the flowers again and covered her mouth with both hands. In her wildest dreams she never imagined 'the guy' she desired wanted her back. She always assumed her weight would be a problem and with the new revelation from Spacey, she wondered how many other guys did she let get away, simply by being more concerned with her weight than they were.

Running after him, she caught him sitting on the beach. Slowly she reduced her height and sat next to him. "You like...you like me?"

He looked at her and shook his head in disgust. "*Liked*. I *liked* you." He focused back on the beach.

She felt her tummy twirl at his use of past tense. "But...why me?"'

He shrugged. "You're beautiful."

She smiled and gasped. "You think I'm—"

"Why wouldn't you think you're beautiful?" He truly wanted to know.

"Because no one ever notices me." She looked down at her body. "That's why."

Finally he got it although weight didn't make the female in his book. "Every woman I ever dated has been plush. It's a personal preference. But what I don't like is sneaky bitches. I've been dealing with that enough in my own family." He stood up and smacked the sand off his rear. "Listen, just...just stay away from me. That's an order." He walked away.

CHAPTER FIVE

The sunshine overlooking the luxurious island was many things as Mason walked toward the plane. He couldn't wait to show his family their new vacation home after he killed Banks but there were many steps in between.

First he had to collect his family from Baltimore. Then he had to get them back undetected. And lastly, after Banks unknowingly flew the Lou family to the destination, he would be forced to kill his forever-best friend, Blakeslee Wales.

When he got to the plane, he moved toward the lower storage area where he would remain hidden. Outside of the ten crates of bottled water, which Mason hid behind on the trip to Wales Island, this area was mostly empty.

However, it was now his responsibility to make it more comfortable for the flight. Flying below deck on the way over, took a lot out of him and he was bumped around more than he could stand. It was so bad that he vomited, lost his bowels and even passed out during the trip over. This time had to be different. So he laid down ten thick beach towels where he would be staying for comfort, along with two ratcheting straps, which he would tie around his waist and connect to the walls of the plane, to keep his body steady on the way back to America.

In preparation for flight, he worked on making his area safe.

Banks just ended a call regarding the status of Minnie. He even sent soldiers to the hospital where Natty, her best friend, was kept after getting shot, but she had since been released and no one saw his only daughter.

His mind was wrecked.

He was about to enter his plane and go to the storage area to get a case of water when Oswalda approached him quickly from behind. "Sir!" She yelled.

Banks' hand was on the latch but he paused and turned around. "What?"

"It's your wife, sir. She's...she's very upset."

By T. Styles

He glared, still annoyed by Bet's behavior over the past few days. "Okay, I'ma get some water and—"

"Sir, I can do that for you." She persisted. "She really wants you now. I would do it myself but she seems to be agitated by me." She shrugged. "I really am sorry."

Taking a deep breath he moved past her and toward the house. When he was out of sight, she entered the plane and walked toward the storage area. With her hands on her hips, she stared down at Mason as he prepared his palette for the flight home.

Sensing he wasn't alone, he jumped up and faced her. He was definitely slipping. He was somewhat relieved it was Oswalda and not Banks but his heart still rocked. "Fuck you doing down here?"

"You mean besides saving your life? Again?"

He shook his head and focused on the palette he was making. "What you want, girl?"

"Banks was on the way inside." She paused. "And instead of being angry with me you should be singing my praises since I stopped him from coming down here."

He looked at her. "Wait...you serious?" The fact that he came so close to being caught, put him off balance. He had gotten so used to going about the large island without being seen that he was too comfortable and allowed his hood guards to come down.

She shrugged. "No reason to lie is it? Especially after what you did to my face."

He walked up to her. "What you want, girl? Because that busted pillow..." he said referring to her mouth. "...well you kinda had that coming." He laughed.

She frowned. "You are evil."

"Ain't about being evil. I'm just not letting nothing get in the way of my plans. And that includes you."

She crossed her arms. "And what plans are those?"

"What do you want, Oswalda? Huh, for me to bust you in the mouth again?" He tied the straps to a hook. "If you asking, I can comply."

She frowned. "You told me the estate will be yours soon right?" She stepped closer. "For you and your family during vacation. Is that true?"

Silence.

"Well?" She continued.

"I have plans for Banks. And not him or any other Wales member will be alive when I'm done."

"Why?"

"My business." He paused. "Not yours."

"Well, if you want my help, I want you to kill my sisters."

He chuckled. "What for?"

"When the sons you told me about come, I don't want any competition." She paused. "I don't understand why I should tell you more than that. Especially since you're not sharing anything with me."

Mason looked at her body and although she was attractive in the face, he was certain that not one of his sons would have her as a wife. "Even if I was interested, why would I murder anybody for you?"

"Because you may want to live here in the future, but first you need to get home. I can be on your team and help throw Banks off your trail until then."

Silence.

"Kill my sisters," she continued. "Please." She stepped even closer. "Now do we have a deal?"

"I'll give you my answer when the time is right. For now you better do your best to stay alive. Something tells me you're in for a fucked up life."

"Why you say that?"

"There's nothing worse than a person making a move on they own kind. Trust me, I know. That type of shit breeds bad karma."

Mason was twisting the arms back on an action figure. He felt too old for them, but whenever he had one Blakeslee seemed to give him attention so he continued to carry them around while hoping...and praying, she'd notice him again.

But this day, his ploy didn't seem to work.

Where was she?

The sun was going down and the crickets seemed to be chirping extra loudly, as if to annoy him. Then there was the fact that he hadn't eaten all day. And so his stomach growled, indicating he was starving. If only he went home he'd see he had a hot meal of spaghetti and meatballs with garlic bread waiting on him but he wanted Blakeslee more than sustenance.

When the door opened to the building, he popped off the steps, dusted the back of his pants off and turned around to see who was coming. To his surprise it was Dennis, her father.

He approached the step. "Sit down, young man."

Mason complied.

Dennis took a deep breath. "When I was a kid, I played with toys like this." He picked up the action figure Mason had been breaking seconds earlier.

Mason nodded.

"Even took to going to bed with 'em." He shook his head.

Mason laughed.

"But it's funny how just having a toy, that was all mine, gave me a false sense of never being alone." He looked at Mason closely. "You know what I mean?"

Mason nodded his head yes, although he was most certainly confused.

"The thing is, my daughter is real." Dennis tossed the toy down. "She's a real person and you can't...you can't throw her away when you done with her." He stared at the young man closely. "She's my little girl and I...I need..."

Mason gave him his undivided attention although he was scaring him. Why was he acting so uptight and what did he want from him?

"Get up." Dennis rose. "Come with me."

Mason grabbed the action figure and followed him into the building. A few seconds later, they were inside Dennis' apartment. The moment the door opened, Mason was hit with loud music and a weird aura. Angie was decorating a Christmas tree even though it was the middle of July. For a second, Mason stood in place and observed the white woman with the pale skin. Her mood was upbeat and extremely happy and yet she was obviously out of touch with reality.

"Oh...hey, Mason," Angie said as a smile spread on her face slowly like a clown. "You came!"

"Just walk to the back," Dennis told him with a firm hand to his shoulder. "Don't say a word."

Within seconds they were in a small room with twin beds. On one of the mattresses sat Blakeslee. Her light cheeks were red and it was obvious that she'd been crying.

Confused, Mason looked back at Dennis but he shoved him inside, closed the door, leaving he and Blakeslee alone.

68   *By T. Styles*

With Mason and Blakeslee now by themselves, he wondered what was the plan. Slowly he walked up to her. "Why you crying?" He was waiting for her answer when suddenly his eyes fell on the action figure with its head popped off on the floor. He rushed up to it and picked up the pieces. "Wait...this mine." Mason frowned. "I was looking for it."

She nodded. "Sorry."

"You stole it?" Mason continued.

"It was in the grass by the fence. I thought you...you didn't need it." She sniffled. "You got a bunch." She pointed at the one in his hand.

It was true.

He sat the toys on the bed. "What's wrong with your mother?" He plopped on the mattress.

She shrugged and sat next to him. "She nice. She just...I mean...she ain't got but half a mind."

He nodded. "So why you crying?"

She looked at the broken action figure. "They broke it. Said they don't want me to play with 'em. They don't want me to be me."

"What you mean?" Mason asked, scooting closer to her.

She swallowed. "How do you...how do you...like being a..."

"Mason?"

She giggled. "Yeah. Sort of."

He shrugged. "I like it I guess. I mean...I like it a lot." His eyes grew sad. "Well sometimes." He thought about his uncle.

She wiped tears away and looked directly into his eyes. Her age may have said young but it was as if she could see right through him. "You wanna ask me something...don't you?"

He nodded. His heart rocked. This was the moment he had been waiting on and yet she appeared more in charge than he was. "Yeah...I guess."

"Ask me," she said moving closer. The sides of their legs touched.

"Can I...I mean..."

"Yes." She giggled again. "You can kiss me." She closed her eyes and he pecked her lips lightly.

His young heart rocked harder and for a moment he felt lightheaded.

She smiled. "You wanna ask me something else too...don't you?"

He swallowed the lump in his throat. "Will you...will you be my...I mean...would it be cool if..."

"Will I be your girl?" She giggled.

70   By T. Styles

"Yeah."

"I will." She held his hand. "And I'll let you...I'll let you do stuff to me. But you gotta let me do whatever I ask too, no matter what. Okay?"

"I can do anything to you?" He breathed deeply. "Anything I want?"

"Anything."

He smiled proudly. "Then I guess we go together."

CHAPTER SIX

Jersey sat on the floor in the bathroom crying after being raped. When she made a decision to leave Mason to go with her foster brother, it was due to fear of what Banks would do to her sons if she didn't get them to safety. The problem with her way of thinking was plentiful.

For starters, she didn't consider who Dragon was as a person. In her mind, she needed to get away and he was the one man she was certain would risk hell and earth to help. She spent the second part of her life with Mason so when she planned an escape from him she went to the man who consumed the first part of her years.

Dragon was it.

Born to Russian parents, Dragon's life wasn't easy. Before migrating to America, his parents were in the midst of a heated divorce. Each vowed to gain custody of Mercer "Dragon" Volkov, but neither was fully equipped to be a parent.

Mentally unstable, when they landed in America, they quickly divorced. Newly separated, and having homes of their own, they went about the art of poisoning Dragon's mind. The plan was

By T. Styles

simple. Whoever Dragon feared more he would refuse to live with, making the other the victor.

It was his mother who struck first. She changed their last names from Volkov to White to infuriate her ex. She then served Dragon alcohol in his juice on Sunday night when he returned from his father. Later blaming her ex-husband when taking Dragon to the hospital for alcohol poisoning. Her ex would retaliate by putting ipecac syrup in Dragon's food, blaming his ex-wife for his sickness.

Before long, it had grown painfully obvious that they were abusing their only child beyond repair, in a sick revenge game. After Dragon went to school officials, complaining that his parents were killing him, he was removed from them both, by Child Protective Services.

And that's when things got sicker.

After bouncing around to a few homes, he was eventually taken into custody by Mr. And Mrs. Smith. On paper they were accepted members of the community. Pillars of society. The epitome of white privilege. But behind closed doors they ran a thriving child pornography business which allowed them to obtain major wealth. What made them dangerous was not their obvious illegal trade, but it was how they lured their prey.

For a year they submerged Dragon into grandeur. Born in Russia, he had never been around luxurious cars or inside a beautiful home like the one the Smith's owned. The moment he laid eyes on the estate, he felt he finally arrived. He loved it so much that he lost contact with his real parents and sank further into the Smith's dark dream world.

But it was over dinner one night that he was presented with an "offer" he couldn't refuse. It seemed simple. He was required to help the family business by having sex with his foster sisters on tape.

And one of the young girls was Jersey.

With his white skin and her African American heritage, they took on the theme of *master* and *slave*. Before long business boomed and Jersey and Dragon were stars with a huge sick fan base. Night after night he had sex with her as she was chained out back in what looked like a log cabin resembling slave quarters. The foster parents couldn't keep the tapes in and one of their biggest fans named the boy Dragon, due to his long penis. Many years later, it didn't take long for

Dragon to feel superior and to even look upon Jersey as his property.

This idea was heightened because although all six foster children participated in the sick business, it was he and he alone who reaped the full benefits. He was doused with expensive clothing, given anything he wanted to eat and was even moved to a private bedroom that was laid out with expensive stereo equipment and a large television.

His demented view of life, made worst by being spoiled and coupled with the damage his parents did to him long before the Smith's got a hold of his soul, turned him into a monster. Resulting in a sex act on camera so brutal, Jersey ran away. Landing a few states over in New York, where she got her rectum and vagina stitched up as a result of the damage from Dragon.

Before long she met her boyfriend. And after Mason killed him, she became Mason's wife.

Dragon's world was rocked. It was only after Jersey left from the Smith's that he realized she was the love of his life. And had he been honest with himself earlier, and asked how she felt, Dragon would have learned that she loved him too. She subjected herself to his abuse for so long, prior to her escape, because in her heart she hoped he would be the man she felt he was under the surface, but that never happened.

Loving him was the single reason she didn't leave the Smith's sooner.

But that was then.

Mason was now.

After subjecting her to another brutal rape in the present, with her sons in the next room, she knew she had to escape or commit murder. There she was sitting on the bathroom floor crying her eyes out and praying for an answer.

And then there was a knock at the door.

"Ma, you okay?" Derrick asked.

"Derrick, you really have to give me my space."

"Ma, why are we here?" He pleaded. "I know something wrong. I can hear it in your voice. Why can't we go some place else? Banks gone now. There's no reason to be scared anymore."

"Derrick, please!"

"Ma!" He yelled. "You gonna make me get up from this chair and...and kill that nigga. Is that what you want? Because you know I will, I swear to God!"

CHAPTER SEVEN

The indoor pool house on Wales Island was cozy as soft R&B music played from the ceiling speakers. Bet and Tobias were in full conversation mode as the night smoothed by.

"...So when I was younger I did a lot of other things too," Bet said to Tobias Nunez. "Some things I'm not proud of, and other things that I consider a part of being young and dumb." They were sitting in a hot tub drinking wine coolers. And Bet was drunk out of her mind as she poured over him.

"I can't see you being reckless," his job was to patronize her more than it was to entertain. And yet if she wanted to fuck he would gladly oblige, but he had to be careful and not make the first move. "You seem so reserved now. I mean, either way it wouldn't be a bad thing but still." He sipped his drink.

"You mean you can't see me dating men for money?" She continued. "Because I had to when I was a teenager. That part is true." She shrugged. "There's...there's a certain lifestyle that I'm accustomed. And only a certain kind of man can appease me."

"Like Banks Wales?" He sat on the bench inside the Jacuzzi.

She walked in front of him, her fifth wine cooler for the day in hand. "There is no man in the world like Banks."

"What does that mean?"

"It means more than you know." She straddled him. "The only problem is, he doesn't love me anymore." She kissed his cheek. "He doesn't *see* me anymore." She cried softly. "And I...I just need somebody to see me. I need somebody to...to kiss me and..." She placed a hand over her chest. "Be there only for me."

Tobias' arms draped the back of the Jacuzzi, like a man on a cross. He was smart. If she wanted the "D" he would oblige but she had to ask. He wouldn't risk his life by touching the boss's wife without her explicit permission.

"I see you, Mrs. Wales." He said. "I've seen you from the moment you stepped through those doors. And if any man fails to see you too, then he doesn't deserve you."

Tears ran down her cheek at hearing the words. Even if they were lies.

By T. Styles

"I just want to know what you want from me," he continued. "Whatever it is, you have to ask."

"I want you to get up and get the fuck out my Jacuzzi," Banks said glaring down at them. He moved so quietly that neither knew he was present. They also weren't sure how much he heard.

Instead of being fearful, Bet laughed as she peeled herself off of the exotic man candy, while sipping her drink.

Tobias on the other hand felt faint as he snatched his towel and hustled out of the Jacuzzi with expediency. Water dripping down his body.

Walking up to Banks while trembling, he swallowed the lump in his throat. "N...nothing happened."

Banks glared.

Tobias ran away.

Bet laughed louder, and it was painfully obvious that she was losing what was left of her mind. "Why you look mad, *boss*? You don't give a fuck about me remember? You don't...you don't care what I do." She tossed the bottle and it shattered on the outside of the Jacuzzi.

Banks removed his sweat pants and climbed into the water, wearing only his boxers. He sat directly across from her so that he could get a look at the woman he gave his last name. "You don't look like the wife of a king. You look like a bird."

"That's right, Banks, insult me more than you already have. You're *soooo fuckingggggg* good at it!"

His stare was fixated and could start a fire. And so she couldn't look at him head on, instead she diverted her stare to her busted drink.

"She was beautiful." Banks said softly. "The most beautiful thing I had ever seen in my life. And she came to me at a time when I was trying to figure things out."

Now she gave him her undivided attention. "What are you talking about?"

"You wanted to know who she was after all this time right?" Banks continued. "So I'm preparing to tell you."

"Why now? You never talk about her."

"My reason was always selfish." He paused as he pictured her face, as if she were a holograph he could see in front of him now. "Because I like her to stay in a place in my head that only I got access too."

She glared. "Go ahead."

"Nikki saw me as I was. In the beginning we were only friends. Living in a city that just took and took and took." He sighed. "Baltimore is the only place on earth where if you're good you'll be great but if you have nothing, it's hell on earth. But she made it better. She made everything better."

"You still love her? Even with her being dead?"

"You never die if somebody loves you."

"Banks..."

He smiled. "The real question you asking is if I love you more than I do her. Don't beat around the bush, Bet. It's obvious you wanna be bold."

She shifted in place because he was correct. "Well?"

"I have never loved a woman more than I loved Nikki." He stared harder. "And I never will."

Bet was frozen in pain. The answer hurt more than she thought was possible. And as she sat in his silence, her face reddened as huge drops of tears filled the wells of her eyes. "You have broken me more than any man before you. And I will never feel this much pain for anyone again."

Banks laughed. "There will be no man after me, Bet. For you I'm it. And the sooner you realize it, the better off things will be."

"If you don't want me, why keep me here?" She yelled standing up. "Why bring me to the middle of nowhere, away from Minnie and Harris? Why cut me down while I'm already cut? Is it simply to see me bleed?"

"So I can build you up." He paused. "To the woman I know you can be. The woman I wanted you to be from the first day we met."

Silence.

"You can't even build yourself up." She took a step closer to him in the water. "Because first of all you're a liar." She paused. "You claim that Nikki was the real love of your life."

"Facts."

"But you're wrong! Because for all the time I've known you, I was forced to watch you try to get away from the *real* love of your life. Mason Louisville." She laughed. "And I sat by day after day, year after year while you fooled yourself that this truth was anything different."

Banks trembled with rage.

"You yell hateful things at me," she continued. "Maybe I deserve them. You even spew words of venom from your lips on a daily basis just to see me cry. But it's all because you can't handle the fact that you killed your only true lover." She

82   *By T. Styles*

laughed. "Oh yes, Banks...I may be losing my mind, but truth is the home of the crazy." She laughed hysterically and then sang, *"Banks and Mason sitting in the tree. K...I...S...S...I...N...G."*

Slowly he rose and slapped her down. When she bobbled in the water like an apple, he helped her to her seat. Standing over top of her, he lowered his height so that they were eye to eye.

She smiled as blood poured down her chin.

Then she spit in his face.

He wiped the glob from his eyelash and grinned. "You will become what I want you to be. You will embody everything I want for my children as their mother. And you will be everything I loved about Nikki."

"And if I don't?"

"Then I will kill you." He stood up slowly. "Oswalda!" He paused. "Oswalda, come in here!" He wiped more spit from his face.

A minute later she stumbled inside the pool house. "Yes...yes sir."

"She's your responsibility now." He stepped out the Jacuzzi and grabbed a towel from the heated rack.

Oswalda raised the white summer dress she was wearing and rushed inside the water. "Yes, sir, of course."

"Fuck you, Banks!" Bet yelled. "I don't need no babysitter! Do you hear me? I don't need a babysitter! I need you to be the man you told me you'd be! The man you promised would always protect and love me! Where is that man? Huh? Where is he? Why do I have to share you with a ghost? Why, Banks!"

Oswalda grabbed her with the strength of many men, sealing her movements as Banks walked away.

"Fuck you!" Bet continued to rant. "Do you hear me? Fuck you!"

CHAPTER EIGHT

Banks was on his plane testing the controls for flight. He would be leaving soon for an eight to ten hour trip and he couldn't wait to get up in the air and back to Baltimore. And he was confident that things would be ready for the next day when Spacey walked into the cockpit. "Dad," Spacey said entering.

Startled at first, Banks looked back at him and focused on the systems. "Son."

"Can we talk?"

Banks sighed. "Spacey, I gotta get ready to—"

"Leave. I know." He cleared his throat. "And that's what I kinda wanna talk to you about."

Banks sighed and motioned to the co-pilot seat for him to sit. Spacey complied.

"Mom is—"

"Spacey, don't worry about your mother." Banks waved him off, already feeling like he knew where Spacey was going. "She's just a little homesick and worried that's all. Once I bring Harris and Minnie back things will be okay. Just trust me."

Spacey scooted on the edge of the seat. "Let me finish, Pops."

Banks nodded.

"Mom...I mean...I think she may be bipolar. I saw this episode on TV once and she reminds me of the way this man was acting. And I know you remember the things that went down at the house, that we thought was mood swings back in Maryland. Well...I'm kinda thinking she needs help. Maybe we should take her to get some in the states before she hurts herself for somebody else."

"I remember the incidents you're talking about," Banks responded. "Like when she was up at 3:00 in the morning making thanksgiving dinner in July that time."

Spacey nodded. "Yeah."

"Your mother is just spoiled and homesick. And the Nunez family will be able to tend to her while I'm gone. Don't worry. You won't have to handle her on your own."

"That's the other part...I want to go." He paused. "With you."

Banks frowned. "Absolutely not."

"Why?"

"Because I need you here. Didn't you just say your mother is sick? And that you're—"

"Pops, the flight is long and I'm the only one in the family who has flown with you on a regular basis. I may not be qualified or have the credentials you do but I know the controls."

"This is not our plane." Banks paused. "Things are different on this aircraft."

"I know. And you're the one who taught me that a car may have different models but the rules of driving are the same."

Banks stood up and turned on the air conditioner to see if it was operating. "Go back to the house."

"But Pops—"

"Now, Spacey! I made my decision and there isn't much you can do to get me to change my mind."

Spacey slowly rose and walked toward the exit. Instead of leaving he stopped. "You always talk about family but you never listen. To any of us. So tell me this, why should we respect you? Why should we even love you?" He stormed out.

Arlyndo had been back to where the Mason estate used to sit many times. Something in his spirit told him that Minnie was there. Somewhere. If only she could give him a sign within the thickness of the trees. "Minnie! Minnie!" He yelled while looking around carefully. "Where are you?" He walked through the forest. "Talk to me!"

Minnie's eyes were closed until she heard a familiar voice. After falling down a ditch, she spent days without food or water. On the fourth day it rained and finally quenched her thirst but at night the forest came alive with very intimidating creatures.

First there were the bugs that crawled into every orifice of her body. Using the warmth of her flesh as havens to stay alive. Then there were the

By T. Styles

hairy critters that attempted to nip at her flesh, taking her body a part bit after bit for nutriment. But it was the vultures that hung in the trees that alone reminded her that she was dangerously close to death.

"Minnie!" Arlyndo yelled. "You there? If you are you gotta talk to me! You gotta let me know where you are!"

When she heard his voice clearer, her heart rate kicked up its pace. But her throat was dry so that when she tried to speak nothing came out. How could she get his attention, when her own body was fighting against her? How could she let him know that he was so close?

It was now or never.

Minnie was certain that if he left, he would never come back, leaving the vultures to do what they patiently waited for. She needed desperately to get his attention.

But how?

After realizing his efforts were in vain, and that he would never find his girl, Arlyndo decided to leave. Why continue to search for her when it was obvious she wasn't alive?

And then there was Mason.

He remembered the day Minnie ran into the woods as if it happened a few hours earlier. Banks had strategically placed bombs throughout their home and detonated them in a systematic fashion. Leaving nothing but destruction in his wake. When Mason sent his soldier Tops to go search for her, Arlyndo reasoned that it was then that the soldier killed her and that his father didn't want to tell him the truth.

Taking a deep breath, and realizing she was gone, he turned to walk toward his car. Suddenly he felt stupid trying to find her in the trees anyway. Who was he trying to be? In his mind it was time to do the impossible. And that was to come to the realization that Minnie was gone.

The moment he made it back home, the plan was to buy a bottle of Hennessy and finish a bottle everyday for a month to get over his broken heart.

Although he was certain it would take longer.

Back at his vehicle, he reached into his pocket and then was stunned. His keys were gone. "FUCK! FUCK! FUCK!" He yelled to himself, while looking on the ground.

Where had he dropped them?

He searched erratically from where he stood and couldn't spot the bright red keychain anywhere. It was time to retrace his steps. The problem was he was so anxious when he first entered the woods that he wasn't sure it was possible. In the end he did his best to remember his tracks while falling deeper into the thickness of the trees. After thirty minutes of a futile search he was headed back to his car when...

"HELP!"

His body froze as he moved toward the sound of a voice. Could it be...Her? At first his steps were slow and then they sped up as he tried to walk nearer to the voice. He was so fast that had he been any quicker, he would've gone over the cliff.

Luckily he didn't.

With daylight as his companion, he was finally able to see the love of his life at the bottom of the ravine. Her body was tossed over some rocks. Her hips were twisted and her leg was extended awkwardly to the left. "Minnie!"

"Lyndo!" She smiled and cried at the same time. "Oh my God you found me! You fucking found me!"

CHAPTER NINE

Derrick rolled into Dragon's bedroom only to see his mother's beaten face. She was sitting on the edge of the bed holding a bottle of Tylenol and she looked drained with life. The rage he felt couldn't be released because he was confined to a chair but it didn't stop his blood from boiling.

When Jersey saw her son's glare she sighed. "Not now, Derrick."

"So this is what it's 'bout now? You getting beat by niggas trying to control you? While I'm in this fucking wheel chair, unable to break their fucking necks! What you expect me to do? Put a bullet in these nigga's heads? Is that what you want from—"

"Careful! One of those men you talking about is your father. He hit me too, remember?"

"I don't care who it is!" He rolled closer. "Shouldn't no niggas be hitting on my mama!" He was so livid he could've twirled around a million times in that chair, doing nothing but making himself dizzy in the process.

Jersey opened the bottle. "Derrick, please don't, I really can't fight right now. I don't have the energy."

"Ma, we gotta get out this nigga's house! We gotta go get some money and stay in a hotel until we figure out what dad doing."

"I don't know where the money is," she swallowed a pill dry and tossed the bottle on the bed.

"What you mean you don't know where the money is?"

"Your father he...he handled everything, Derrick. I guess I never felt a need to ask for my own money because he bought everything I wanted. Do you actually think I would still be here if I had any cash? We're stuck until Mason gives us our next move. Unless you have some money tucked away that I don't know anything about?" She sighed and waited for his answer. She could tell by his face he was broke too. "And even if we did have money I still don't know if it's a good idea to leave. Banks may be on the island now, but it doesn't mean that he didn't have his men on the lookout for us."

By T. Styles

"What you 'spect me to do?" Derrick continued. "Sit by and watch this pig-white-son-of-a—"

"Stop!"

"Stop what?"

"Dragon is a monster," she stood up and opened a dresser drawer, removing fresh socks. "There's no denying that so I won't bother trying. But he was made that way." She placed the socks on her feet. "And I still believe, somewhere deep inside of him, that he loves me." She took a deep breath. "But I'm so tired...so tired of people hating each other because of how they were made. I'm tired of feeling hate for people myself...I'm talking so much hate that I can react in ways I don't think you could ever believe."

"What you mean?"

"I'm capable of evil, son. I'm not perfect. Especially when it comes to keeping you guys safe. I want a chance to love and I want a chance to—"

RING! RING! RING!

Jersey reached for her cell phone on the bed and answered. "Yes."

"Is this Jersey Louisville?" She looked at her son. "Yes it is. Who's calling?"

"We believe we have your sons Patterson and Howard Louisville in police custody. You need to come to the precinct."

"I don't understand," she paused. "They're adults. Why couldn't they call me?"

"Let's just say that they're too inebriated to speak to anyone, and this call is simply a courtesy."

Just at that time the front door opened and closed. Within seconds Dragon appeared behind Derrick in the doorway. Believing he had something to do with whatever was going on with his brothers, Derrick looked up at him and glared.

Dragon responded by grabbing the handles on the wheelchair and rolling him out of the room, closing the door in his face. Derrick punched the door in defiance but it didn't matter.

He was on the outside.

"I'll come as soon as I can," Jersey said to the caller, while her eyes rested on Dragon. "Just please...please make sure they stay safe." She ended the call and continued to stare at her foster brother.

She knew what happened and she knew why it happened. The move that was made was the

96

type she always feared from him. That in the end, if she refused his advances, and didn't fall in line before Mason returned, that Dragon would ruin her life and the lives of those she loved.

And she was correct.

Dragon plotted to break her down from the day she didn't let him touch her body without force a few days ago. It was another reason he took the weakest of her sons out on an excursion, knowing full well that Derrick would never fall for such a trick. It was to a party where whores poured liquor down their throats and then cried rape in the night.

He set up everything.

After ending the call, she walked up to him and placed her arms around his waist. When it came to her sons, there was nothing she wouldn't do, including give him her body willingly. "Okay, Dragon." She whispered.

His chest rose and fell heavily. "Okay what?" He looked down at her with disdain.

"Okay...I'm willing to do whatever you want." She paused. "Just...just get them out of jail. Please."

He took a deep breath. "I want to hear the other words, my love." He stroked her hair.

She looked up at him, with tears in her eyes. "Okay. I'll stay. And submit to you and you alone."

He took a deep breath, one that rocked a few curls out of place.

He won.

For now.

CHAPTER TEN

Banks hung in the doorway of his bedroom suite quietly. From where he stood he could see the bathroom door open and Bet sitting in front of Oswalda in the large tub. Both had on bra and panties and Oswalda was stroking Bet's hair softly as she hummed.

Bet looked at peace.

For a moment he thought back to when Oswalda said Bet wanted him when he was on his way to the plane to get water. When he asked Bet what she needed, she appeared to be clueless. He figured she was losing her mind.

Within seconds, Bet seemed to relax and hum along. For some reason, seeing her calm put him at ease and he had hope that maybe she would return to the woman he wanted her to be, although he had nothing to base his hopes on.

When he caught himself smiling, he cleared his throat and turned around. Just as Spacey was walking into his room, which was some ways down the hall, he followed and hung in his doorway.

Sensing he wasn't alone, Spacey looked at him but remained silent.

"How are you?" Banks asked.

Spacey shrugged. "Fine I guess. We 'bout to swim on the beach."

"Who?"

"Me, Joey, Cassandra and Emetine." His response seemed uninterested.

Banks frowned. "You like one of those two?"

"Not really." He shrugged. "But I'm bored."

Banks smiled. "I figured."

Spacey frowned. "Why you say that?"

"I know what kind of girl you like, Spacey. Oswalda was one of the reasons I settled on the Nunez family."

Spacey's eyes widened. "How would you know? I never brought a girl to the house."

"Don't you realize I think of everything in advance? Can't you understand that even the things you assume miss me, I find out about?" He paused. "Like I said, I know your type. I know Joey's type. I know Harris' type too. Nothing misses—"

"What about Minnie?"

By T. Styles

Banks sighed. "Unfortunately I know what kind of man she settles for. Hopefully I can change that with time."

He opened his drawer. "One day you won't be able to figure us all out. And even if you do, it won't matter."

"As long as you are a Wales, it will always matter."

"And what does it mean to be a Wales?"

"It means that you're royalty."

Spacey slipped into his trunks. He wasn't interested in talking to his father any longer than he had to. "Whatever you say, Pops."

"Just make sure you don't stay out too long tonight," Banks said, taking a deep breath.

Spacey frowned. "Why not?"

"You coming with me tomorrow. And I need you rested."

Spacey walked over to him slowly. "Wait...I can go? I thought you said you wanted me to stay here with—"

"I know what I said," he responded cutting him off. "But I heard what you said too. Sometimes I think you're still a kid when I have to remember you're a man." He placed a hand on his shoulder. "We leaving at 5:30. So be ready."

Spacey hugged him tightly. "Thank you! Thank you for trusting me. I won't let you down."

Oswalda's feet were caked with sand as she rushed toward the towel shack by the beach. She had to be careful that no one was watching but the news she held was of the utmost urgency.

When she made it to the shack, she walked back toward the furthest left corner where Mason lied hidden behind some racks. His eyes were closed but she knew him enough to realize he was far from sleep.

"What you want now, girl?" He asked, lids still shut tightly. "I was just getting into some good sleep."

"How do you do that?"

He opened his eyes and glared. "How do I do what?"

"Know I'm here before you even see me?"

"What you want?" He repeated, uninterested in schooling anyone.

She cleared her throat. "I was taking care of Mrs. Wales when I walked into the hallway and up on a conversation Spacey was having with Banks."

"Get to the part that concerns me."

"I overheard Banks telling Spacey that they're leaving tomorrow."

He rose. "Are you sure?"

"I wouldn't come by unless I was certain." She paused. "Now what about our agreement? Are you going to kill my sisters or not?"

Mason smiled as he thought about seeing his wife and sons again. Yes he had plans for the island and most of them entailed killing Banks and taking the property from him. But none of it would matter if his family wasn't with it all.

"Mason," she continued. "What are you gonna do about my sisters?" She stepped closer. "Remember? You promised to kill them for me."

"I don't recall giving you an answer." He stood up and moved near her. "But trust me, when I get back here, you'll get everything you asked for and more."

CHAPTER ELEVEN

Banks had taken flight.

He was at eight thousand feet and approaching ten thousand to reach above the clouds. Because it was a clear sky he could fly VFR, which meant *visual flight rules* versus IFR, which meant *instrument flight rules*. That option was mostly conducted at night when not a structure was in sight.

Just being in the air, put him at extreme ease. It was certainly the only place he truly felt at home. From the co-pilot position, Spacey looked at him as he controlled the mechanisms on the plane with the ease of a professional. It always made him feel good to see his father use such an amazing talent, which was one of the reasons he loved to fly with him.

"I know why you love it up here," Spacey said looking out the large window ahead.

"Because it's beautiful," Banks responded.

"Nah, I know the real reason."

Banks put the flight in cruise and looked over at him. "Okay...I'm listening."

By T. Styles

Spacey gazed through the cockpit window at the spectacular view again. "Up here, everything seems so small. Troubles. People. All of it."

Banks nodded.

"And up here, nobody can judge you for being...you." Spacey continued.

Banks frowned. "Why'd you have to go fuck it up?"

"I didn't mean it that way...it's just...I mean...I been thinking 'bout the island. I been thinking about all of it and I think I finally get you. Flying and having a place of your own means an escape."

"You don't know shit about me, Spacey. You see me, but you don't know shit. Buying the island and moving us there was all because I wanted to protect my family. All because I wanted to make us safe. And if you think of it any other way it's a disrespect to me and my legacy."

"Even now?" He paused. "I mean think about it, Uncle Mason is dead. Why do we still have to be there? Alone? There's nothing to escape from, except you."

"Drop it, Spacey. Before I regret why I allowed you to come." Banks got up and stormed toward the back.

Mason lie below deck on the plane with his cell phone pressed against his ear. The strap was wrapped around his waist and connected to the plane and the towels made him somewhat comfortable. Since the weather was good he wasn't rocked around as much and for that he was grateful.

Normally cell phones wouldn't be able to be used but the state of the art plane had Wi-Fi built into its features and as a result he could talk to his son.

"Derrick, I want you to be straight up with me," Mason whispered. "What's going on at home? Why hasn't your mother been answering my calls?"

"You forgot she was mad at you?"

"You think I'm stupid?" Mason responded. "Had she not picked up for me the other day I would've assumed we were still on bad terms but she did answer. Now what's going on?"

"I'm kinda scared that something may happen to ma."

"Finish." Mason paused, nostrils flaring. "Whatever you tell me will stay between us. The last thing I want her to do is get upset with you. So trust me when I say you can talk to me." He paused. "Is it about Arlyndo?"

"Nah...he's been gone a lot lately. I think he still looking for that girl."

"She dead." He said assuredly. "Tops took care of her. Now what is it about?"

"Patterson and Howard."

Mason frowned. "Go 'head."

"They locked up."

Mason's breath felt trapped in his throat. Although he realized he didn't tell them where the emergency stash was, it wasn't because he was trying to hide money from them. It was mainly because when Jersey first made a decision to run, he was unprepared because she drugged him. Wasn't able to tell them about the safe with his stash. But still, any of his men would've gladly given them a stack if they were hard up.

So why were they in jail?

"What happened? Did they rob somebody?"

"I don't know. Something about rape and shit. But I think Dragon had something to do with it."

RAPE! He thought.

"Dragon? Why would he...I mean..."

"He a cop."

If Mason could've dropped out the plane he would have. When Jersey finally told him about Dragon, after he pressed her for days on end, she never, not once said he was police. Hood Rules for Mason's line of business and Dragon's made them natural enemies.

Why would Jersey make such a move?

Was she that scared of her own husband?

"Listen, don't tell your mother you told me anything. I'll take care of it all."

"Dad, you gotta be careful. This white nigga different."

"I got us." Mason assured him. "Just let me handle things from here."

CHAPTER TWELVE

They were in a hotel room.

The doctor was checking on the fresh cast he made for Minnie's leg earlier that day. When he was certain it was steady and with time would repair the broken limb, he stood up and walked over to Arlyndo. The Louisville family was the bane of his existence and he wanted to tell its youngest member how he felt.

Instead he said, "She should be fine. She cannot leave the bed though. She has to keep her hip still for a few days. The device I have her ankle in will keep it in place." Not only had Minnie broken her leg, she also dislocated her hip. Luckily the doctor was able to reset it at Minnie's painful expense.

He looked down at her again. She was wearing a long muumuu style yellow dress. It was the only thing Arlyndo could find, since she couldn't wear pants. "Thank you doctor," she smiled.

"No problem." His smile was fake and far from endearing. He focused back on Arlyndo. "You must find a better place and time to contact me. I can't keep jumping whenever somebody in the

Lou family gets shot or hurt. I have a practice to run. And you're family is killing business."

Arlyndo glared as the doctor laid into him. When he was finished he moved closer. "I think you need to remember who I am. And who my father is. Threatening me in any fashion is bad for your health." He stabbed a finger into his clavicle. "But you know that already don't you?"

"I'm not saying it's a problem coming tonight. It's just that I'm a very busy man and—"

"You will come whenever I or anybody in my family hits you. Don't fuck with us. Don't fuck with me."

The doctor swallowed the lump in his throat. "I'm sorry. I just—"

"Get the fuck out," Arlyndo walked to the door and opened it wide. The doctor moped toward it. "And Doc, keep this little visit between us. Don't need nobody from my family knowing about me and my girl."

The doctor nodded and exited quickly.

When they were alone, Arlyndo walked up to the bed and sat next to her. He placed a warm hand on her thigh. "Hungry, bae? Can I do anything for you? Or anything to you?" He asked sexually.

By T. Styles

She giggled. "How many times you trying to feed me? Because I know you don't fuck with big girls."

"I want you to eat as much as you can. You lost a lot of weight." He paused and took a deep breath. Thinking about where he found her still messed with him. Although he saved her life, he was trying repeatedly to come to terms with the fact that had he been a little later, she would be dead. "Minnie, I can't believe...I can't believe you were...there all those days by yourself."

She squeezed his hand. "I'm fine. I just...I think your father was trying to kill me. And I know you don't wanna hear that but he sent somebody after me. Somebody very scary and very nasty. This nigga was even jerking off while watching me run for my life. What kind of person is that?"

He stood up and walked across the room. Tops looked weird to him too. Leaning against the wall he said, "I think you right. That's why I didn't want the doc telling my father you were here. At the same time I didn't know who else to call to fix your leg and hip." He ran his hand down his face. "I don't understand why my father would try to kill you though. He helped raise you. I just...I don't understand none of it."

She looked down at her legs and tried not to cry. "I shouldn't have left my parents. I should've listened when they said to stay with them."

He frowned. "But if you had we wouldn't be together right now."

"But I wouldn't be hurt either." She cried. "Look at me, Arlyndo." She threw her hands up in the air. "I fucking fell off a cliff just because Mason sent a pervert in the woods to kill me. I should've listened because they knew and—"

"I said you were right, damn!"

She looked at him. "I'm sorry."

"Don't be. It's just fucked up to hear that's all," he continued.

She reached out for him and he walked toward her, standing on his knees. They held hands. "I love you...I won't ever forget what you've done for me, Arlyndo. I promise. If you didn't look for me...I'd be done. But...now it's time to let my family know I'm alive."

He glared. "What that mean?"

"It means that I'm grateful that you—"

"You think I'm a bird don't you?" He frowned.

"What you talking about?"

By T. Styles

"You think you can have me save your life, only for you to leave me again? Is that it? Why the fuck did I pull you back from death just for you to kill me by walking out my life?"

"Arlyndo!"

"Arlyndo what?" He yelled standing up. "What do I have to do to convince you that you should be with me? Huh? Your own father didn't find you. I did! You know where he at right now? On that island! Chilling." He pointed at the door. "They left you but you don't give a fuck do you? You still wanna be with people like that just because you share their last name."

"Arlyndo, I have never wanted anybody more than I wanted you."

"*Wanted*?"

"You know what I'm saying." She cried. "Stop trying to twist my words around. Why does everything have to be on ten when we fight? Why can't you just take what I'm saying and leave it at that? I don't want to be without you. I just want to...I mean...please let me call my parents."

"No."

"Why though?"

"Because they'll take you from me again. Uncle Banks knows how to find niggas. The moment you hit his phone, he'll probably have it traced and they'll drag you away. And I can't suffer through that shit no more."

"You said yourself they left for the island. What makes you think they'll come back for me? Especially after everything I've done. I just wanna hear their voices. And tell them I'm okay. I know they're worried. Plus I sent a letter that...that I gotta tell dad about."

"Nah."

"Arlyndo!"

"I said no!" He yelled louder. "Now I have you here for a reason. To keep you safe from my people and yours too." He pointed at the floor. "And if you don't like my way so what!" He shrugged. "There ain't shit you can do 'bout it." He grabbed a plastic bag off the chair and stormed out the door.

CHAPTER THIRTEEN

Banks landed the plane smoothly back in the states.

The moment he opened the cockpit, twenty of his men who awaited his arrival, surrounded the aircraft to greet him. They were all excited to see him but having heard the news that he was a woman, they examined his features a little closer than usual, each trying to determine if there was truth to such an incredible story. And soon, although they scrutinized him heavily as he moved toward his vehicle, they were coming up short identifying one feminine trait.

In the end most believed the rumor to be a lie.

At least they hoped.

Rev walked up to Banks and shook his hand, as well as the hand of Spacey. "It's so good to see you, sir," Rev said sincerely. "It's good to see you both."

Cliff, the man who saved Banks' family and who was originally one of Mason's men, was also in attendance.

Banks shook his hand as well.

"Good to be home," Banks admitted to them both. "Any word on my daughter?" He asked Rev right away.

"None. But the fact that we haven't heard anything good or bad...well...to me means she's still alive."

"What about Arlyndo?"

"He's been off the grid lately." They walked together toward Banks' truck, with his soldiers following. "I heard he was upset when she went missing and took to the bottle hard. But I can't be sure because no one has been able to find him."

Banks nodded. "Well keep an eye out. The moment you hear something let me know."

"Got it."

Banks opened the door to the Escalade that was waiting on him and turned around. "And keep an eye on this plane too." He observed it and sighed. "I can't risk something happening to this one. It's the only link between me and my family on that island."

"I'm on it."

By T. Styles

"Fuck," Mason said to himself as he peaked through a window from the plane. "How the fuck I'ma get off this bitch now?" When they landed, he was hoping he could rush out once Banks left the area and get picked up by his men.

He was wrong.

Banks wasn't going to take a risk that someone from the Louisville organization wouldn't trash another aircraft, despite believing Mason to be dead. Taking his cell phone out he made a call. "Derrick, we landed but don't send a ride for me just yet."

"We were on the way though," he paused. "Why I gotta wait?"

"Banks got the plane surrounded. It's gonna be hard but I'll come up with a plan."

"But why wait? Even if the plane surrounded?" He paused. "I say we send somebody and kill every nigga lined up."

"And we just may have to do that. But for now, hold off. I need Banks to assume I'm dead for as long as possible. I'll find another way."

Banks sat in Harris' lawyer's office while waiting for the status. He hadn't shaved and so his beard irritated him beyond belief. But there was no time for grooming. He needed to know the deal about his son but so far the information he was given wasn't good.

"I'm not certain, but I'm pretty sure they will deny his bail," the attorney said, sitting across from Banks at his cherry wood desk and leather chair. "And you should be prepared for that too."

"I'm not understanding." Banks leaned closer. "He's never been in any trouble. And this crime is so ridiculous. Why is he even in that FCI prison when he hasn't been convicted of anything?"

"The holding facility was overcrowded. So they sent him to the closest federal facility that had a camp to await trial." He explained. "Tampering with a mailbox is a federal offense. And one they take seriously. I mean, what was he doing in there anyway?"

Banks slammed his hand in his fist. "I wish I had an idea. I didn't want him admitting any

118   *By T. Styles*

guilt, even with being on a cell phone. So he never told me why he was arrested. And I don't want people knowing he my son because he'll be bait." He took a deep breath. "But I need to get him out of there. He's not built for this type of situation."

"Are there any illnesses that I can let the judge know about? Like cancer? Or childhood ailments that require care? Since his record is clean it may be what we need to get leniency."

Banks searched his mind. "No...we don't...we don't have anything that would warrant them letting him out."

"Well unless we give the judge a reason, there really isn't anything I can do about it." He sat back in his large leather chair. "I'm so sorry."

Banks stood up and walked toward the door. Before walking out he doubled back. "I don't have to play games with you. You know what kind of man I am."

The lawyer frowned. "Exactly what are you saying?"

"I'm saying that I heard about attorney's robbing people in my position, because the law is already against us. But if you think for one second I'm gonna let you take my money and leave my boy stranded, you don't know me."

The attorney nodded. "I understand. And I would never try you."

"Get him out. I don't care what you have to do."

"I'll do my best," The attorney said.

"Do better."

Banks sat in his office on the phone. He didn't feel like talking to his wife but he knew she would be driving Joey crazy if he didn't open up the lines of communication. "Things will be fine, Bet."

"You keep saying that but how do you know?" She paused. "For sure?"

"Stop asking me the same shit over and over!" He shuffled a few documents about Harris' situation on his desk.

"Banks, I had a dream." She was breathing heavily, and he could tell she was on the verge of exploding. "It was a terrible dream. That we buried Minnie and when I went to kiss her in the casket, it was Harris' face instead."

"Don't be crazy!"

By T. Styles

"Find my kids, Banks. Find them and bring them to me."

Three of Banks' men stood outside of two trucks in the airport that held Banks' plane. They saw the stakeout for the boss as easy money, considering they didn't have to do anything except make sure no one harmed the aircraft.

"I'm telling you them niggas lying!" D.C. said. "I know for a fact that nigga ain't no bitch."

"How can you be sure though?" Red Cap responded. "They got all kinds of shit to make them look like niggas nowadays."

"So hold up," Shorty responded. "They can have a dick too?"

They all laughed. "I don't know 'bout all that. If anything she probably carrying a dildo or some shit like that," Red Cap responded.

"You better stop saying *she*!" D.C. warned pointing at him. "You gonna mess around and say it around the boss and get fucked up."

Red Cap waved the air. "Ain't nobody saying it around Banks. He won't ever catch me slipping like that. I'm not stupid."

"Well still don't say it around me," D.C. said harsher. "I'm serious. I ain't trying to pick up on your dirty habits and—"

"We expecting company?" Shorty asked pointing at the cars approaching the plane.

"Nah," Red Cap responded removing his gun. "But gear up! It looks like we under attack."

Standing at the foot of the bed, waiting for Joey to give the word, she could see his foot peaking out from under his expensive thread count sheets. She stared at him as he rubbed his hand over his muscular bare chest and eyed her with lust.

"I'm waiting for your order," she said. "But if you don't mind...I'd like to do a little something different tonight."

Her accent sent chills down his spine and he was certainly intrigued. "Aight...do you, mami."

By T. Styles

"Close your eyes."

"Then I can't see you."

"Maybe that's the point," she replied.

When his eyes were closed, she lowered her height and suckled his big toe.

At first he was grossed out but soon his dick got rock hard. In control, Cassandra licked her tongue in between each toe and then slurped each as if they were candy. Her breasts bounced against one foot as she cared for the other.

"Damn, so I got myself a freak," Joey responded.

"That was just the opening," she said as she slid his covers off and rose on top of his dick. Her wet opening swallowed him whole and he couldn't pull her off if he tried.

She wanted it...bad.

Just when he was satisfied being inside of her, She rose up again and quickly locked her tongue and her lips around his thickness.

"Please say my name," she replied.

"Cassandra...fuck...suck that dick, Cassandra."

As she heard her name, her tongue slid down to his balls and she kissed, licked and sucked his nuts ever so gently. He could tell giving head was her passion and he was happy for it.

"Fuck, Cassandra...why you doing that shit so good?!" He asked looking down at her.

As she went to work, Joey closed his eyes and let his imagination continue to roam on every freaky thing he ever saw. Every time he drifted off thinking about another nasty bitch, she would do a trick with her tongue to remind him that she could handle him alone.

"Cassandra...just like that...keep that shit just like that!" He pawed her head to maintain his hold as he pumped softly into her mouth.

When the dick was so hard his veins pulsated, she crawled on top of it and allowed it to part her strawberry colored pink lips. He was so horny that he fucked her as hard as boxing gloves hitting a bag.

"Say my name, Joey," she begged.

"Cassandra...Cassandra...fuck...shit!"

Not being able to handle much more, Joey flipped her over on her back and tore into her harder. Spreading her legs wide, her ankles brushed his earlobes as he rammed deeper into her slushy pussy.

By *T. Styles*

As her vanilla colored breasts bounced up and down, he lowered his face and sucked each one as if saying hello. Before long it was obvious he wouldn't last and she knew it too.

"Cum in my face," Cassandra begged. "I want to taste that shit."

Going with the flow, he pulled out and bust all over her lips and black hair.

When he was empty, he lay next to her, trying to catch his breath. "Nice," he said.

She giggled. "That's all I get?" She scooped his nut from her cheeks and sucked her fingers until it was all gone. "Nice?"

"That's all I got."

She rolled on her side. "I'm glad I could please you."

"Please me?" He said looking at her cute face. "We fucked so much tonight you have to be carrying my seed."

She rolled over on her stomach. "I hope so."

He smiled at her and then frowned. "Hey, how come you want a baby so bad?"

She took a deep breath. "You really have to ask?"

"Yeah. Every time we go at it, you bring up having a baby. Any other time I'd be fucked up with infant talk but you make sure I'm good first."

She sighed. "Because if we are going to be here, on this island together, I want to have something to live for. I mean, it's almost like we have to populate the world all over again. Here, we can be anything we want. Like your father said."

Joey thought about the word 'father' and he was briefly reminded that Banks was a woman, and that the Nunez family had no idea. But he preferred it that way. "So you really wanna be with a nigga?"

"Don't like your use of the word but yes." She smiled. "I want you to officially make me yours. But if you don't, *Con el tiempo serás un recuerdo.*"

He frowned. "What does that mean?"

"In time you will be a memory."

"You'll be a memory too if you don't make me a sandwich."

She frowned and fell on her back. "Mr. Wales, you have to be clear...do you want a slut or an employee?" She rolled over and squeezed her ass until it bounced repeatedly. "Because you can't

By T. Styles

have both. But let me give you some advice...I'm better in bed than I am in the kitchen."

He slapped her cheeks. They jiggled.

Sure he could've demanded her, but it would have ruined the day. Plus since Spacey wasn't interested in Emetine, he had plans to fuck her the next day. So he didn't want to spoil the mood knowing full well she would be heated later.

So for now, he would let her breathe.

"I be back." He got dressed and walked toward the door.

"And Mr. Wales..."

He turned back around to face her.

"Make me one too."

He nodded his head and dipped out.

A few minutes later he was in the kitchen making two ham sandwiches. When he realized he hadn't seen his mother all day, he decided to stop by her room before going back to Cassandra for round four.

With his plate in hand, when he walked toward his mother's suite, he saw her crying on the bed. The lights were out but the moonlight coming inside the window provided a soft glow. Something felt strange. Oswalda was standing on her knees behind her whispering something in her ear. As if she were silently mouthing a curse. She was so close that it looked weird and put him in immediate discomfort.

"What's wrong, ma?" He tried to look inside but the room was somewhat dim and made it hard to see.

When Oswalda saw him she rushed toward the doorway, stepped out and closed it behind herself. "Hello, sir. How are you?" She looked at his plate. "I see you're hungry. Can I do something else for you?"

"What's going on with my mother? And why you close the door like that?"

Oswalda moved a little and cleared her throat. "She's fine...she just...I mean...she hasn't been feeling—"

"I'ma be straight up," Joey stepped closer. "I don't like you. Ever since your sisters told me you tried to snitch when we were in the bowling alley, I made a decision that me and you gonna have problems."

She frowned. "Why you say that?" She placed her hands on her hips. "I would never snitch on anybody. I just wanted to be sure we are doing our jobs and not just having fun. I mean, it's what your father paid us to do right?"

128   *By T. Styles*

"I still don't trust you."

"You haven't gotten a chance to know me."

"You sneaky. And I'm from Baltimore, where we can spot sneaky fat bitches from miles away. And if you think I'm gonna let you fuck up my mother's mind then—"

Oswalda abruptly pushed the door open. The knob stopped short of slamming into the wall. "If you think you can do so much better, go in!"

He frowned. "What you doing?"

"It's easy. I've been taking care of your mother, alone. But if you think you can do it yourself, feel free. I don't have any problems just cooking and cleaning around here."

"Stop acting like a—"

"Your father asked me to help her but she cries. Every minute. Every second. Every night. And I get no break. So if you wanna trade places, maybe I'll go fuck my sisters and leave you both be."

Joey looked into the door. His mother's eyes were red and he thought about what Oswalda was saying. No he didn't want to be full time with Bet, but it wasn't because he didn't love her. It was strictly because there was nothing more painful in the world than seeing your mother cry.

And he wasn't built for the responsibility.

"You don't act like a caregiver, or a maid. Who are you really?"

She smiled.

"I'm watching you." He pointed in her face.

"What do you wanna do? Because you still haven't answered my question."

He swallowed the lump in his throat. "You take care of her." He paused. "For now."

She walked into the room, and slammed the door in his face.

Banks' men, who were protecting the plane embraced for the worst when they saw the cars approaching. Luckily for them all were slightly relieved when they realized it was their peers, more of Banks' men.

"Nigga," Red Cap said tucking his gun, as he approached one of the two cars. "At first I thought ya'll wanted heat." He dapped up Johnson, one of the four men who exited the vehicle. "What ya'll doing here?"

By T. Styles

"We here for relief." Johnson replied.

"Good, because we been out here all night and I'm starved," Shorty admitted.

Although Red Cap and Shorty were at ease, D.C. stared at them with more scrutinizing eyes. "How 'come Banks ain't say we were supposed to get off? Normally he would hit one of us up and say something."

Johnson looked at D.C. and then at the three men he rolled to the landing dock with. Taking a deep breath, he wiped his hand down his jaw. "I don't know, maybe you gotta ask him."

D.C. pulled out his phone. "Maybe I'll do that."

"You know what, fuck this shit," Johnson released his hammer and his men quickly followed suit. In the end they killed D.C., Red Cap and Shorty in cold blood on the landing strip.

When he was done, Johnson walked over to the plane and knocked three times on the side. Within seconds, Mason opened the plane's door and came out. "What took ya'll niggas so long?" He frowned. He smelled of urine and was off balance after the flight to America but at least he was on solid ground.

"Banks had us doing something earlier," Johnson admitted. "But we here now though."

Mason walked down the steps and dapped him before looking at the men at his feet in confusion. "Thought I told ya'll I wanted this done without bloodshed? To keep the nigga Banks off my track? That's why I got you instead of my guys." He shook his head. "If I wanted dead niggas I could've used my own men."

"Sorry," Johnson shrugged.

Mason shook his head. "You know what...pick up the bodies and put 'em in the trunk." Mason walked toward one of the cars they pulled up in. "And lets get the fuck outta here."

"Aye, Mason, we can still work for you right?" Johnson asked. "'Cause I know we fucked up tonight by laying these niggas out, but I don't wanna work for her no more."

Mason frowned. "Her?"

"Banks." He laughed. "She a bitch right?"

The other men thought the slight was hilarious too but Mason wasn't feeling it one bit. Besides, he didn't tell Johnson the news, so that meant the word spread around the city.

Mason's jaw twitched. He always felt disloyal since he put his closest men on to the fact that Banks was trans. At the time he felt it was his best move, but now he wasn't sure. "Pick up the

132   *By T. Styles*

bodies and lets get the fuck out of here." He got inside. "NOW!"

CHAPTER FOURTEEN

The morning sky was threatening rain...

Dragon yawned deeply after stepping out of the bedroom where Jersey lied inside. Derrick, the only Lou son not locked up for rape, or missing in action like Arlyndo, was heated about his brothers. With Patterson and Howard being in jail, and Arlyndo being only God knew where, he alone was left to deal with his mother's downfall.

Dragon walked up to him, while scratching his pale bear chest. "Where your brother?" He yawned. "The little one?"

"Why? So you can get him locked up too?"

Dragon grinned. He felt the temporary cripple was a joke who was unworthy of his respect. "You can't be serious."

Silence.

"If you think I would do something purposely to get my nephews locked up you don't know me or your mother." He scratched his chest again, leaving red tracks that went away seconds later.

"There's one problem," Derrick glared.

"And what's that?"

"You not our uncle. And I don't know why you on some revenge shit with my moms but I know who you really are. And I want you to realize that you not gonna get away with it. Us Lou's always get our revenge. I promise you that."

He laughed. "I think your mother did you a major disservice by not telling you boys who I am."

"Enlighten me."

"I will." He paused and sat next to him on the sofa.

Derrick tried to move over but the limited use of his body due to the wounds he sustained along with the amputation, made everything futile. He hated his body right now, and worked everyday to get most of his mobility back.

"Your mother and I grew up in and environment where we had to fight for each other." He shrugged. "That puts us in a unique situation that not a lot of people can understand. She was weak and I was her protector."

"Like a master?"

Dragon laughed. "Don't let the white skin fool you. It would be a big mistake."

"All I know is that since I been here, I done watch my mother get bruised up. If you supposed to protect her, explain that part to me. Because I'm not understanding right now."

Dragon rose and walked toward the kitchen. "I think you want to talk to your father about your mother getting beat up first before you come see about me." He looked at him with hate. "Remember?" He opened the cabinet and grabbed coffee grounds. "She showed up to me with those bruises." He pointed at him.

"So you felt like you could add to 'em? That's your thing? Beating a person already in pain?"

Silence.

"I love your mother. Deeply. And sometimes, when people love each other they argue and fight." He shrugged.

"Where your bruises though?"

He laughed. "Don't worry, we seeing our way back to each other. Soon everything will make sense." He placed the grounds into the coffee pot. "Give us some—"

"When my father gets back, he's gonna murder your ass."

Dragon poured water into the pot. "He can try. But I guarantee—"

KNOCK! KNOCK! KNOCK!

By T. Styles

Dragon frowned while Derrick eased into his wheelchair.

"You expecting company?" Dragon asked.

"Nah."

Dragon stepped out of the kitchen and hustled to the door. Once it was open, he was surprised to see Mason on the other side, with his hands clutched in front of him making one big fist.

Naturally the cockiest of all Lou's walked inside without an invite. "Where my wife?" He continued to step into the man's home.

Dragon placed a firm hand on his shoulder to slow his move. "Hold up!"

Mason stared at the hand for what seemed like an eternity, until Dragon realized his violation and removed his paw slowly.

Derrick on the other hand sat in the background smiling.

"Where she at?" Mason inquired. "I'm not gonna ask again."

Dragon sighed. "She's asleep. And I suggest you come back later when—"

"When what?" Mason moved closer. "You put me in a position where I gotta kill you? Because you need to understand something clearly...I'm not leaving without what belongs to me." He glared. "And you can take that however you want." He looked at his son. "Go to the truck."

Derrick smiled. "You sure you don't want me to stay?" He looked at Dragon and then his father. "This dude foul, Pops."

Mason looked down at him. "Nah, because I don't predict there'll be a problem. Not today anyway." He focused back on Dragon. "Because this a smart man. And smart men understand when they're being given a break. Especially after putting hands on niggas wives and shit. Ain't that right, *COP*?"

"Oh...you talking about *me* putting my hands on her?" He pointed at himself. "Or *you*?" He stabbed a finger in Mason's chest and Mason dropped him with a closed fist.

It took Dragon a few seconds to realize what happened. And when he did he wasn't happy about it at all to say the least. Back on his feet, he stepped up to Mason and glared at him with hate. It was obvious things had escalated quickly.

"I'm gonna return the favor soon enough," Dragon promised.

At that moment, Jersey stepped out the backroom and her timing could not have been better. Because Dragon was five seconds from making his next move.

Which would have ended in cold-blooded murder.

"Mason..." she said, her body trembling. "You're back." She ran up to him and wrapped her arms around his neck tightly. "Oh my God you're back!"

"Go get in the truck," he said, eyes still on Dragon. Just seeing his wife's face had him a new level of angry. It was a level reserved for men who witnessed their mother's get punched in the face, while knowing there was nothing they could do to stop it. He now felt bad for what he put his sons through the day he struck her himself.

She separated from him. "What about my stuff?"

"You don't need nothing you got in this bitch."

She looked at Dragon. "Dragon, I—"

"GET IN THE TRUCK!" Mason yelled. "AIN'T NOTHING ELSE TO SAY TO THIS COP, 'CEPT BYE!"

Jersey quickly obeyed.

Derrick followed.

With the door hanging open due to their exit, Dragon looked outside and saw a bevvy of men looking toward the house. Under the graying sky, he could tell by the bulges on their hip lines that they came prepared to attack.

And so he smiled. "Why you still here?" Dragon asked sarcastically. "You got the girl. So bounce."

Mason nodded. "I'ma do all that. But you gonna stay away from my wife too." He pointed at him.

"You see...that's where your threats come up dry."

"For your sake you better hope that's not true." Mason bopped out.

By T. Styles

CHAPTER FIFTEEN

After picking up Howard and Patterson from jail, before Dragon could stop the wheels from turning due to being salty, Mason drove down the street mostly in silence. Derrick was in the front seat while the duo that felt the need to hang out with a traitor the night before, played the backseats.

Jersey was at the house waiting on her family.

"What were ya'll thinking?" Derrick asked, breaking silence. "I gotta know." He looked back at his brothers. "What about that mothafucka had ya'll thinking shit was sweet to hang out with him? Wasn't you paying attention to how he was doing ma? You know a nigga in a wheelchair and need your help. But you didn't even care!"

Howard looked at Patterson and both of them held their heads low. They knew the bait he was trying to walk them into and they refused to bite.

Derrick glared. "So what, now ya'll wanna fake silence?"

"Ain't nobody gotta answer you, nigga," Howard said.

Big mistake.

"Well answer me!" Mason roared at them, looking at their faces from the rearview mirror. "Why would you trust a man in a uniform? Did you forget who we were?"

Patterson and Howard stared at each other.

"ANSWER ME!" Mason roared.

Both swallowed.

Patterson parted his lips. "Dad, ma said he was family and I—"

"Does his skin match ours?" Mason said. "Have you ever met this man a day in your lives prior to a month ago?"

They both shook their heads no.

"So what exactly about him made you believe he was family?"

Patterson looked down. "But he had girls at the party," he whispered. "I thought he was good."

"Bitches at a party?" Mason shook his head. He was so disappointed he couldn't contain himself. Mainly because their ignorance was a direct reflection on his lack of teaching. "It's always 'bout shit that don't matter with this family."

"We sorry," Patterson continued.

"Well that ain't good enough," Derrick interjected. "'Cause while you were too busy

142   *By T. Styles*

fucking with chicken heads, ma was getting whooped by old boy."

"What?" Patterson yelled.

"You heard him!" Mason followed up. "In my absence you were supposed to protect your mother. Not worrying about some funky ass females that can't do nothing for you the moment you get up off 'em!"

Silence.

"Is ma okay?" Howard asked.

"Does it matter?" Derrick responded.

Silence.

Not another word was uttered.

Ten minutes later they pulled up into one of Mason's nicer properties in Owings Mills, Maryland. As they piled outside of the car, it became evident that a lot of mistakes were made during their time with Dragon. But if Mason were honest, he would have to admit that their downfall started with him.

Once inside the house, they saw Jersey sitting on the couch biting her nails. The moment they walked through the door, she rushed up to her sons and hugged them tightly in relief. Both Patterson and Howard felt like shit when they saw her newly bruised face but it also felt good to be in her arms.

Mason allowed them the time, but when they were done he said, "Sit down." He paused. "Everybody."

Each took a seat in the living room. Patterson and Howard on the floor while Derrick remained in his wheel chair and Jersey on the couch. Mason on the other hand remained standing.

"We got a situation." Mason said.

They all nodded.

"Dragon is gonna be a problem. I saw it in his eyes."

Jersey looked away and then back at him. "I don't think so. I mean, he did let you go. Maybe he realizes that if he hurts my family I'll hate him forever. What he wants is a relationship with me."

"Nah." He said. "I forced his hand. Didn't leave him much choice and because of it he's going to be looking for a way to get back at me. To get back at us. This not good." He took several breaths. The fact that Mason had yet another problem to deal with, when his first enemy wasn't annihilated yet, agitated him.

"Why you say that though, Pops?" Howard asked.

By T. Styles

"Because he police. And I'm a hood nigga. So it's natural that we must beef."

"I'm so sorry," Jersey said, understanding the power of what she'd done. "I just...I just wanted my sons away from the war and—"

"I don't blame you." Mason said. "I blame myself."

Everyone looked at him as if he was crazy. Mason did a lot of things but apologies were generally not one of them.

"So now we have to be on the lookout." He paused. "That means we not going to be able to get money on the streets. Basically the family business is on hold."

"So this situation is like it was with Banks," Howard said. "Where we got to hide? Cause we been through this already."

"It's worse." Mason said. "Banks helped raise every last one of you. The nigga Dragon don't want nobody in this room but your mother. And he police. That makes him worse."

Everyone looked at one another.

"Where can we go?" Howard asked.

"I'm not sure. But first somebody tell me where the fuck is Arlyndo?"

CHAPTER SIXTEEN

I t started to rain...

And it fit the mood perfectly as Arlyndo pulled up in front of an apartment building in Pikesville, Maryland. His heart pumped as Charlie, a cute red bone who loved him since the day he ate her coochie in the back of a movie theater, ran toward his car to avoid getting drenched.

"It's crazy out here!" She said jumping into the passenger's seat, shaking her umbrella. "The rain came from nowhere!" She leaned over and kissed his cheek.

He smiled, but was tense as he looked at her.

Her grin washed away. "Wait...you okay?"

"Yeah..." he cleared his throat. "Yeah...but what you wanna do tonight?"

She frowned. "We talked about this already on the phone. I thought you were taking me to—"

"Get something to eat," he said remembering what he told her. His mind was so fucked up that it was tough keeping his thoughts off Minnie. She was truly all he cared about and he wondered what she was doing at the hotel. Alone.

By T. Styles

"Yeah...lets...lets get something to eat." He pulled off.

"Can we go someplace and talk first?" She placed her seatbelt on.

He leaned his back toward the window as he piloted the car. "Yeah...what about?"

"Everything, Arlyndo."

"Okay...I know a spot."

She smiled. "Thank you. I know you don't like this *'girly shit'* but it will make me feel better. I don't want whatever we doing to be just about sex anymore."

"I get it...for real."

He continued to drive but would look her over every so often. He examined the features of her hair, her face, her chest and even her legs. When she caught him checking her out he cleared his throat and removed his gaze.

"It's okay," she wiped her hair behind her ear.

"What you talking about now?"

"I like when you look at me." She touched his leg.

He tensed up.

For some reason waiting to find out what she wanted to rap about had him heated. Add to that the fact that the silence caused him to swim in his own thoughts and it was driving him mad. "Look, you might as well tell me now."

"But I thought we were—"

"I don't like games." He paused. "So tell me."

She took a deep breath. "I need you to finally choose me. I need you to not fake like you want me, but only when you and Minnie fight. I need...I need you to make me your girl, Arlyndo. No more sneaking around, causing me to hear from the city that ya'll back together. I want—"

"You right."

She frowned. "What you mean?"

He laughed. "I said you right." He shrugged. "Don't get me wrong, I love my girl but she be faking like she don't want me know more." He shrugged. "And I give up a lot for her. So I can't with the disrespect. I'm looking for something regular."

Her eyes grew wide as she smiled brightly. "For real, Arlyndo?"

"You wouldn't be in my car if I wasn't thinking about being serious." When his phone rang he glanced down at it. His mother had been calling him back to back, but what shocked him was that the number was coming from his father's line.

By T. Styles

Was he home?

Catching the fear on his face she said, "You okay?"

"Yeah...uh..." he maneuvered the car unsteadily. "Um...we should go to my house."

She frowned. "I thought you said it got burned down."

"It did. But we still got acres of land on the property so I figured we could talk more there." He nodded toward the back of the car. "Got some blankets in the back and everything."

She smiled so hard wrinkles touched the corners of her youthful eyes.

Ten minutes later they were along the side of the road. The same place his car was parked where he found Minnie earlier that day.

When the engine was cut off he trembled.

"What's wrong?" She asked touching his arm.

Arlyndo pushed the car door open, jumped out and fell on his knees. Within seconds everything he ate earlier came out in a heaping pile of green mess on the grass.

Confused, Charlie jumped out of the car and rushed up to him. Placing her hand softly on his back she asked, "Is everything okay?"

He wiped his mouth with the back of his hand. "Yeah...I...I'm sorry."

She smiled. "For what? Just 'cause you're sick? It's okay, Arlyndo. I'm not that shallow."

"Nah...I'm sorry for this..." Arlyndo whipped a gun from his waist and shot her in the belly. When she dropped to the ground he shot her again in the same spot. "I'm so sorry," he cried. "I'm so fucking sorry."

BANG! BANG! BANG!

Five minutes later, after dressing her in Minnie's old clothing, which he had in the plastic bag he took from the hotel, he drug her into the exact spot he found Minnie. She had the same build. And the same skin color. Her hair was different from Minnie's but he was certain his next move would make that problem a non-factor.

Removing a can of lighter fluid from his back pocket, he doused her with the liquid and set her body on fire.

When her corpse went up in flames, he ran away.

By T. Styles

After spending two hours trying to find a way to get out of bed and out the room to use the phone, Minnie was surprised when a housekeeper walked inside. Mainly because she remembered hearing Arlyndo tell management that he was not to be disturbed in his room.

At all.

But the maid must not have gotten the message. And as a result, she was on a mission to knock all the rooms off her list.

She was a Hispanic woman with young eyes but an extremely old and wrinkled face. "Oh, I didn't know you were in here," she said upon seeing Minnie lying in the bed.

Minnie pulled herself up as best she could. "No...please...please come in!" Minnie yelled.

"No...I can come back later when—"

"Please, clean my room!" Minnie said more aggressively. "Now!" She didn't mean to come across as brash, but she was trying to do all she could to get the woman to stay.

After a few more seconds, the woman looked at her and shrugged. "Okay...I'll clean bathroom and take out trash."

As the woman entered and exited the room, removing linen and taking out trash, Minnie spotted a bulge in her pocket. "Excuse me, can you let me use your phone?"

The maid stopped and looked in the direction the hotel phone should be but it was pulled from the wall. Arlyndo had snatched it out the same night they arrived, to keep her from contacting Banks. "My phone?"

"Yes...it'll only be a minute," Minnie pleaded.

"No...guests can't use my personal phone. It's against rules." The maid grabbed her bucket from her cart and walked into the bathroom.

"Please."

"Why?" The maid paused. She studied the weird girl with the slightly bruised face and drew a conclusion. And then she looked at the cast on one leg and her ankle contraption on the other and figured her assumption could be off. "Are you a sex slave or something?"

"No...I...of course not!" The last thing Minnie wanted was the maid to call the police. Because although she wanted to get a hold of her family, she knew if the police were on to her, then it would take no time before Mason found out too.

And she was still very, very afraid of him.

"Then no...you can't use my phone." She proceeded to clean up the bathroom while humming.

What now?

Minnie had to be smart.

If she presented herself as fearful to the maid, the police would come and she would be taken into custody, only to be spotted by Mason or one of his men later. So she thought back to her devious-bratty days and just like that she had a plan.

"What are you doing in this country anyway?" Minnie asked.

The woman frowned.

"You heard me. You're here for what? To take our jobs. To take our men? To take our money." She shook her head. "It would be so much better if you and your people were gone."

The maid glared. "You don't know nothing about me."

"I ain't gotta know nothing about you, bitch! I know you shouldn't be here when you not born in this country. I know that much! I don't like the president but I hope he builds that wall."

Within seconds the woman ranted off in Spanish some extremely hateful things. She was so angry that spit flew from her mouth as she grabbed her work supplies and exited the room.

Despite the woman's anger, Minnie was sure her plan would come together.

All she had to do was wait.

CHAPTER SEVENTEEN

Banks sat in his car next to his mailbox at the end of the driveway, while talking to Rev on the phone. "What you mean the men not at the plane? I gave them specific orders to stay until relieved."

"I know and I don't understand what happened, sir," Rev said. "I went to the airport like you asked but nobody was on guard. But don't worry. I sent five more men to make sure the plane will be protected and trust me, they aren't going anywhere."

Banks sighed and ran his hand down his face. It seemed as if everything was falling apart, ever since he made a decision to leave for Wales Island. "Did you check with their people? To be sure they okay?"

"I checked everywhere for them. Nothing."

Banks shook his head. "Something feels off. What about Johnson?"

"That's what I wanted to bring up to you," he paused. "When I called to tell him I needed him to stand guard earlier today, after the others left, I found out his phone is off. He must have a new number. I don't trust him."

Banks sighed. "If you see him, kill him."

"Without reason?"

"There's always a reason. If he changed his phone number without telling me, then he's not for the team."

"True." He paused. "And what about Cliff?"

"Right now he's done good by me and my family, with getting them to safety that night. Just give him light work to wet his appetite. Don't put him near anything major."

"Got it." Rev paused. "And we on our way back to Mason's land now. To check for Minnie again."

"Yeah...I was over there earlier but came up short." He paused. "Smelled a fire but figured it'll be like that for a minute, after the bombing. I guess it's the actual house still letting off that odor."

"I don't know about that," he paused. "That was a little over a week ago. Maybe something else was on fire. The fumes should be out of the air by now."

"Maybe...just let me know what you find."

Banks ended the call, grabbed his mail and walked into the house. Thumbing through the envelopes, he was shocked to see a letter returned to sender due to unpaid postage.

It was addressed to the FBI.

Confused he walked to his bedroom and opened its contents. "What the fuck?" He recognized Minnie's handwriting instantly. The paper was on letterhead from SWEETHEART INN. The same place he had her held when she escaped the house.

To Whom It May Concern:

My father Banks Wales is a drug dealer. He has been selling cocaine in and around our home for as long as I can remember. He will be flying out of the country soon. I'm letting you know now because he has all of the credentials to fly, due to never being caught committing a crime. So he will be able to leave undetected.

I hope you get him before he can get away. He wants to take me too but I want to stay here.

Please help.

Minnesota Wales.

Somehow after reading the letter, Banks had walked into his office, although he didn't remember how he got there. Confused at what he just read, he flopped in his chair. The pain he felt was the worst kind imaginable. He couldn't believe Minnie had attempted to alert the FBI when all he wanted was her happiness. They have had their spats in the past...

But this...

This was the fourth most painful moment in his life. The first being the loss of his mother, followed by the loss of Nikki and then the murder of Mason.

He was still thinking about the betrayal when Shay walked into the office. In the past, he purposely tried to avoid her since he returned home but it didn't work. She always found a way to be up under him.

He left her over two hundred thousand in an account in her name which he planned to replenish as needed while he was at the island, so she could finish college and live her best life. But that was the extent of his relationship plans for her. Besides, how could he look her in the face, when he witnessed Stretch murder her mother only to take him out later?

"Sir."

"What is it?" He sighed.

"How are you?"

By *T. Styles*

Banks looked at her for a few seconds, somewhat in disbelief. He would've bet money on the fact that she would ask about her parents. Or even about Harris. But this inquiry threw him for a loop to say the least.

"I'm fine."

She walked further inside. "I know, I mean, I know you're leaving me here. And I...I understand if you don't want me with you anymore. But I guess I'd like to know...uh...do you know where my parents are? Do you know where my mother is because leaving me alone...this...I mean...seems unlike her don't you think? Seems unlike my father too."

There it is.

"I don't know where they are, Shay." He looked down at his desk and shuffled a few papers around, including the letter of Minnie's betrayal. He had known Shay as a child, whom he seldom had to interact with, so this convo was a bit heavy and out of the ordinary. "I'm sure they will—"

"They dead."

He looked up at her.

"Ain't they?" She continued.

Silence.

"When I was little, my mama used to tell me she'd bring me a Rottweiler puppy here, all the time." Huge tears rolled down her face as she spoke. "And everyday even up to a few months ago, I believed her. Held onto the hope because I wanted it so badly. But as the years went by..." She sat on the sofa across from him. "...Hope turned to hate. For my own mama. Because it wasn't good for nothing no more." She wiped tears away. "So if you ever cared about me...even in the slightest, I would appreciate the truth. No more fake puppies. No more fake hopes."

Banks sat back and ran his hand down his face. She was smarter than he'd given her credit for and suddenly it became obvious why Harris liked her so much, despite Banks' recent veto on their relationship, after finding out about it a few days ago.

After all, they were siblings by blood so Banks could never sanction their union. He would have knocked it down months ago if he had been wiser.

"Your father killed your mother. And I killed him." He paused. "It was business, but I'm sure it doesn't make your pain any less."

She nodded rapidly as tears flooded the wells of her eyes. What he was shocked about was that even though she was distraught, no sound exited her lips. Instead, she took a deep breath and wiped her tears away.

"Okay...okay..." She wiped them again. "My daddy always told me that in war you lose soldiers,..." she cried more, and this time it was a bit harder for her to pull herself together. "...And I guess it's my time now." She took a long deep breath. "But you see...now you owe me."

He frowned.

"Don't worry...I ain't got no use for no more money. I plan to be a doctor someday anyway and I'ma have plenty of that." She sniffled. "But you gotta give me something else. Something more valuable to me. Something I want more than life itself."

"What is it?"

"Harris. My Kirk. You gotta take the veto away, sir. It's only right that we should be allowed to be together now."

Banks didn't have a lot of time for her threats but she was right about one thing. She was a child and he did owe her, especially since he had a part in making her an orphan.

But to him her price was too steep.

"My son's not for sale. Sorry. The answer is no."

"Then raise me like your own. And I'll let him go."

"My own?"

"Make me Shay Wales."

He sighed and thought about her new request for a few minutes. Silence stood between them but neither felt uncomfortable. "Okay," he said.

She took a deep breath mixed with tears. It was a sweet but bitter juice.

"But don't take your hands off of Harris just yet," Banks pointed at her. "I need him sane until I can get him out of prison. Be what he thinks you are to him. But you and I will both know that when he is home, this thing, whatever it was, is done."

She wiped tears away. "I'll cut Kirk off the moment he's out of jail. And he won't know of our agreement."

She left directly thereafter leaving Banks alone to ponder the daughter who betrayed him and the son he had just betrayed. He knew his luck was about to run out, due to everything he'd done. He just wanted a bit more time.

By T. Styles

He was so stressed that the next morning he awoken to find himself still at his desk, asleep, until his cell rang. He jumped up and answered. "Hell...hello."

"Sir...I have...sir..."

"What is it, Rev?" He could hear the panic in his voice. And it immediately put him on edge too.

"The fire...the odor you smelled...it was Minnie."

Banks paced the floor. "I don't understand."

"She...she's dead." He paused. "We found her body in the woods. Was wearing the same clothes you told us she wore the day she went missing. And I—"

Banks hung up and dropped to his knees.

After getting drunk with Emetine last night Joey slipped quietly out of her bedroom in the servant's house and into the mansion. Normally he never stayed in their home, never wanting whichever sister he was sexing to assume it was more than sexual. He had also yet to tell Cassandra that he wasn't feeling her anymore.

Still, he wasn't much worried. Banks had left him in charge and he saw this departure as an unspoken statement that he alone ruled and could do as he pleased.

Besides, he was a Wales.

Wearing grey sweatpants and no shirt, he was about to see what the matriarch of the Nunez family prepared for breakfast when he stopped at his living room. Nothing appeared the same. Every piece of furniture had been rearranged, right down to the pictures on the wall.

Rosa and Ives, smiled when they saw him approaching and met him halfway. She looked guilty and as always used her smile to deflect and throw people off.

"What's going on?" Joey yawned, pointing at a picture where Jay Z usually hung. "Why you got Spanish Jesus on the wall instead of Jigga?"

Rosa glared. "That is not Spanish Jesus! That is Saint Jude!"

"And what he doing on my living room wall?"

She took a deep breath and smiled. "We only put him up while your father is away. We had him up before you moved here, before you met

By T. Styles

your new home and it protected the island. It's only right while your father is gone now, that we put the Saint up again. To protect over us. To protect over you too."

"Nah, tear all this shit down," He ordered waving his hand. "Put it back the way we liked it."

"But Mr. Wales is not here."

He glared. "Pops ain't gotta be here for shit to stay the same. I'm here. My mama here. Now put Barack letting that little boy touch his head back on that wall or whatever, and Jay back on the other. And put the furniture back the way we had it."

She glared.

Ives did too.

Joey stepped closer to them. "Yah hear me or not?"

She stared at him a bit longer and then blinked a few times. "Sure, sir, whatever you say."

He walked away.

"Con el tiempo serás un recuerdo," she whispered, as if it were some dreaded curse.

He stopped and turned around slowly. "What you just say?"

"Anything you want, sir," Rosa responded with her chiseled smile again.

The thing was he knew she was lying. Cassandra had already put him on to what the saying meant. What she actually said was; *in time you will be a memory.*

Rosa repeating what Cassandra had before, told him a few things. The main one being that they talked about his family being a memory a lot, using those exact words.

He just had to find out why.

What was also clear, in the moment, was this...something was wrong with the Nunez family.

Something was *dreadfully* wrong.

By T. *Styles*

CHAPTER EIGHTEEN

Arlyndo walked into the hotel to see Minnie watching television. He was pushing a wheel chair and in the seat he carried McDonald's breakfast and fresh clothing. "Bought you something to eat and wear." He handed her the food bag.

"Thank you so much." She took it from him quickly. "I needed more clothes." She opened the food bag. "Plus I'm starving."

He looked at her hard.

Something felt off.

Why wasn't she yelling at him for leaving her alone overnight? Why hadn't she told him how much she hated him? Even from where he stood he could smell the feces from the diaper he placed on her since she couldn't use the bathroom on her own.

Where was the outrage?

"You okay?" He asked as she tore into the sausage McGriddle.

"Yeah...why you say that?" She chewed more and sipped orange juice at the same time. "I'm fine." She shrugged. "Gotta be changed though."

He nodded. "Cool, because—"

KNOCK! KNOCK! KNOCK!

Arlyndo whipped is head toward the door and back at Minnie. "What you do?"

She shrugged and answered with a mouth full of food. "I been here all night by myself. Stuck in the bed. What could I do?" She placed her juice down on the table.

"Anybody come to the room? This morning or yesterday?"

"No." She lied. "Why you asking me a bunch of questions?" She bit her sandwich.

KNOCK! KNOCK! KNOCK!

Arlyndo stood at the door, frozen with fear.

After some time Minnie whispered, "Arlyndo..."

Silence.

He stared at the door as if it were going to reveal its secrets without him answering.

"Arlyndo!" She put her sandwich down.

He looked at her.

"Maybe you should open the door?"

Slowly he turned toward it. "Who is it?"

"Management." A male voice said calmly, but with authority.

"What the fuck?" He said to himself before opening the door. He was mostly relieved it wasn't

By T. Styles

the police or his parents. He had done all he could to avoid them and it appeared that as of now, his efforts worked.

But on the other side of the door, there was an angry maid standing next to an older black man wearing a suit. "Are you Mr. Peterson?" The Manager asked.

"Uh...yeah." Arlyndo responded to the fake name he'd given so he wouldn't alert people, mainly his family, where he was.

"Well this message is for you." He stepped closer. "I want you and your lady friend over there to be out by..." he looked at his watch. "...3:00pm." He wagged a finger at her. Minnie looked away. "And not a second longer."

"Hold up...I paid the room up for a month." Arlyndo replied.

The Manager dug into his pocket and handed him a wad of money. "That's all you paid, including the money for the days you used. Consider it a parting gift and an expression to show how much we really want you out."

Arlyndo counted the money. It was all there plus a little cushion. "Why though?"

The manager looked at Minnie and back at him. "Hotel policy." He stormed away, leaving Arlyndo stuck.

The maid stayed a second longer and smiled sinisterly at them before she too followed.

Confused, Arlyndo slammed the door shut. "You know something 'bout that?" He pointed at the door with his thumb.

"Why you keep looking at me? I can't even move, remember? Maybe we have too much activity coming in our room...with the doctor and all." She picked up her sandwich and ate again.

He scratched his head and flopped on the edge of the bed. "Nah...I don't have nobody here but the Doc."

"Now what?" She asked.

"We gotta get outta here. Get another room I guess.

"Well, we better hurry up."

After wiping her down and changing her clothes, he unhooked her ankle from the traction device and helped her into the wheelchair. Then pushed her out into the lobby. "I'ma go get the car." He walked away but quickly returned. "Don't forget, if something happens crazy, or you try to get away, my father will find and kill you. It ain't

170   By T. Styles

like he hasn't tried before." He paused. "Remember one thing...you're safer with me, Minnie. You know that right?"

"There ain't no place I wanna be but with you, A. You saved my life. I swear to God it's just you and me. Stop doubting my loyalty and love."

He looked at her intensively and walked away. The moment he was out of sight, she rolled her chair around the lobby. When she spotted two girls texting on cell phones, she rolled toward them as quickly as her arms would push.

"Excuse me, but can I use your phone?" She asked the one with the long braids.

The girl frowned. "Sit the fuck down some where with all that dumb shit," she laughed. "You ain't using my phone, bitch. So you can roll off with it?"

Since she was already seated she knew the girl was dumb but it was all she could do to not pull up by one arm and slap her in the face. "Please! It'll be quick." Minnie persisted. All she wanted was to alert her parents that she was okay, even if she wasn't returning home anytime soon. "I need to use that iPhone."

"Why though?"

"Because I...I...I mean—"

"What are you doing to my guests now?" The maid she disrespected yesterday questioned, walking up behind her. The same woman who was responsible for getting them thrown out of the hotel.

"Nothing...I was...I mean...trying to use...I mean...the cell."

The maid glared. "You were asked to leave. Now don't make me get security because you don't know how to listen." She paused. "Now go!" She pointed at the exit.

Feeling and looking dumb at the same time, Minnie rolled away and up to Arlyndo who had walked back into the lobby. She was nervous because she didn't know he came back so quickly. Or how much he heard.

"What was that about?" He asked.

She was relieved. He was still clueless. "Nothing." She said under her breath.

"So why that bitch look mad now?"

"Cause I cussed her out for throwing us out. I couldn't leave without giving her a piece of my mind, you know me 'Lyndo. But lets get outta here though." She looked at the maid again who was still staring. "I think she may call the cops."

Joey was asleep in bed and Emetine was behind him, also knocked out. She was a light snorer and didn't break up his rest too much. But when he felt someone in his room, he opened his eyes, only to find Cassandra standing on the side of the bed, smiling.

Her stance was off-putting and awkward and so he frowned. "What you doing in here?" He yawned. "Thought I told you not to come in my room anymore without—"

Emetine screamed loudly behind him.

Joey looked back at her and said, "Fuck wrong with you?"

She pointed at her sister and it was at that time that he saw that the middle of her white nightgown was red, as blood eased from between her legs and dripped onto the floor.

Cassandra passed out.

Two hours later, Joey was pacing in front of Cassandra's room, when Oswalda walked out and stood in front of him. "How is she? I mean, she okay?"

"She lost the baby."

Joey placed his hands on the sides of his face and dropped them quickly. It wasn't until that point that he fully understood the gravity of what he'd been doing. He had allowed his status and power to use a beautiful woman for his own sexual desires, and now she had a miscarriage.

In a matter of speaking, his first-born child.

"I didn't know she was...I mean...she didn't tell me she was pregnant. How she even lose it?"

"Maybe stress." Oswalda shrugged. "I mean, I don't know how it would be if I had to witness somebody I love fuck my sister everyday." She shrugged once. Pierced her lips and shrugged twice more for a Latin effect.

"Aye, watch what the fuck you say to me!" He said stepping to her, a long finger in her face.

"Or what?" Tobias asked walking up behind him. "Let's assume she doesn't watch what she says, just what the fuck are you going to do about it?"

Joey stepped to the side, and backed a few feet away from them. When he glanced down at Tobias' waist, he swore he saw a bump.

Was he packing?

"What's up with ya'll?" Joey asked suspiciously. "Now that Pops gone ya'll acting brand new. I mean, who are ya'll really?"

"We the Nunez's," Tobias said with a wide crazy smile. "What's up with you?" He rested his hand on his hip, to let him know he was ready to pull the weapon.

"Something's off. I know that much," Joey replied.

"I think you the one who's acting strange," Tobias said. "And before you think it wise to tell your father anything, think about what you did to my sister. How you got her pregnant and then started fucking my other sister instead. Your father seems honorable enough and I'm sure he wouldn't want to hear how you willfully defiled her body." He shrugged. "If I were you, I'd keep this between us. I know we won't say a word, will we sister?" He looked at Oswalda.

"I'm not saying a thing," she smiled sinisterly.

Feeling like he was in the company of devils, slowly Joey walked away, keeping his eyes on him the entire time. A few hours later he called his father. "Hey, Pops."

"Hello, son," Banks said, his voice as heavy as a city block.

Joey immediately noticed misery in his tone. "Are you...are you okay?"

Banks sighed. "Just a lot on my mind," he paused. "But how are you?"

Joey took a deep breath, preparing to tell it all.

"And your mother?" Banks continued.

Instead of unleashing all that had gone down on Wales Island recently, Joey took a moment to take in the tone of his father's voice fully. He could tell something was happening and didn't want him burdened with anything extra, especially since he didn't have facts.

And then there was the situation with Cassandra.

Tobias was right.

If he told Banks about Cassandra and her miscarriage, how would that make him look to a man he adored?

So he took a deep breath. "Everything on the island is perfect, Pops. Mom's getting rest and is happy."

By *T. Styles*

"Wow...really?" He sounded relieved.

"Yep, and I...I guess I just wanted you to know I got things over here. Take as long as you need."

CHAPTER NINETEEN
MONTHS LATER
DECEMBER 23RD

Mason sat on the patio of one of his homes. The weather was frigid and although it was the holiday season, he was far from being in the mood as he talked to his brother in jail. "It's crazy." Linden said, the weight of the prison in his voice. "I didn't care about nothing at first. All I wanted was revenge and—"

"On who?"

"I'ma be straight, I wanted revenge on everybody, even you. I wanted you to pay for...for...everything because before we reconnected, when you took Banks' side, I felt my anger was part your fault."

"I ain't feeling you on that." Mason frowned. "Me and you beefed because I wanted to make money with—"

"Banks...the same nigga you beefing with now."

Mason remained silent because he was speaking facts."

By T. Styles

"But that wasn't the only reason," Linden continued. "I was also mad because when I left New York, a lot of promises were made that didn't go answered. I thought things would be different when I moved with Pops. And I guess I was still a nigga who wanted his father in his life. Instead, after Banks, he was killed. And since he was your friend I blamed you."

"I never saw him like you did." Mason picked up his beer and took a gulp. The cold kept it chill. "He...he let shit happen to me on his watch that..."

"I know about your uncle." He paused. "And I'm not gonna even lie, he was wrong for not keeping an eye on you."

Remembering the sexual abuse Mason endured as a kid had him feeling uneasy. He never thought about those times because they were too painful to analyze. And this moment was no different. "You know what, I ain't even talking about this shit." He paused. "Not now or never."

"I get that too."

Mason took a deep breath. "So all this...the hate you got for me, it's always been about Pops? That's the reason you don't want a visit now in prison?"

"Nah. That's because I ain't telling nobody I'm here. Me and Tops don't even conversate no more. I feel like it's smarter that way."

Mason nodded. "Probably best on this end too. That cop Jersey grew up with been fucking with everything, man. Haven't been able to move on the streets for months. All because he mad my—"

"Watch what you say. This a cell but they can still be listening."

"My bad." He burped. "Been a minute since I talked about any of this shit. Guess I'm just venting."

"Listen...I never spent what you gave me. Not all of it anyway. Go see Pops and you'll find it near but do it as soon as possible. If you can tomorrow."

Mason frowned. "What about you? Won't you need that for later?"

"You good for it." He paused. "I just want you to take what you need."

"Why?"

"Don't look a gift horse in the mouth." He paused. "Besides, you family. Get the paper."

When Linden ended the call, Jersey walked out and sat next to him. "I heard what you said to Linden."

By T. Styles

"So you eavesdropping on my calls now?"

"Kinda," she sighed. "It's just that you don't talk to me that much so I never know what's going on. If I don't sneak around I'd be clueless." She paused. "And...I'm sorry about Dragon still being in our lives. Messing with business and..." she took a deep breath.

"You sorry about everything ain't you?"

"Nope...I'm not sorry for taking my sons away. At the time, when you were beefing with Banks, I really thought that was the best thing to do."

"I know." He stood up, and removed a pack of Black & Mild's and lighter from his pocket.

"Any plans? On our next move?"

"Linden gave us some money which should help out a little." He lit one and put the pack and lighter back.

She frowned. "He did?"

"Yep...that frees up some cash for protection and shit like that. That way we don't have to keep tapping our stash." He blew smoke into the air. "And we can pay what we owe niggas." He sat down. "I do have some good news. One of my friends said he spotted Arlyndo at a hotel in Arlington. If he's there I'll get him, grab Linden's money and we'll go to Florida or something."

"I don't know why he's ignoring us," she paused. "This doesn't seem like him at all."

"I don't know either. They say he was with some female in a wheelchair. Probably one of his birds."

She took a deep breath. "What about Banks?"

"I think I'ma leave him alone." He inhaled smoke. "This issue with Dragon made me realize I'm done with all of this fighting and shit. I just want to get my family from up under that cop and move on with my life."

Her eyes widened. "Are you serious?"

"Yeah, I'm—"

Before he could finish, she wrapped her arms around his neck tightly. He almost burned her by accident. "I prayed for this. Prayed for the moment that we would be able to let the war with Banks go and you give it to me when I least expect it."

He smiled. "If you prayed you won. As long as he doesn't make a move on me or any other Louisville, I'ma let the nigga Banks breathe. It's as simple as that."

By T. Styles

Joey walked through the house to check on his mother. He found her in the bed, in the dark, looking up at the ceiling. Concerned, he took a deep breath and sat on the edge of the mattress. The glow from the hallway light allowed him to see her clearly.

"Ma..." he gazed up at the crystal light chandelier. "What you looking at?"

She turned her head and focused on him, a light smile spread across her face. It almost appeared that she was slightly drunk, but he knew for a fact that she hadn't touched alcohol in months. Besides, he'd hidden it from her long ago.

"Hello, son."

He touched her hand. "Ma...you good?"

She shook her head and looked back upwards. "Get out, Joey. Please." There was still a light grin on her face and had he not heard her directly, he would've thought she said something else.

"Ma," he whispered. "What's wrong?"

"Please, Joey. Just go."

He stood up and walked out.

Moving slowly down the hallway, with his head hung low, he heard angry talking from afar. Although the Nunez house was outside of the estate, if they were on their porch, voices could be heard from one of the guestrooms within the Wales' Mansion. Something he discovered the day he and Emetine decided to get freaky and hide away from her family one night.

Since the Wales clan preferred that the house be cooled with natural air coming off the beach, most of the windows were left opened until midnight.

Curious about the tone of the voices, cautiously he walked into the dark guest room and up to the window. Standing on the side of the pane to prevent from being seen, he squinted and looked at the front of the Nunez home. Rosa, Tobias and Ives were standing on the porch, talking to a Latin man in a white linen suit. He looked powerful and dangerous, evident by the two-armed guards in military attire behind him.

Who were they?

Joey slid down the wall, grabbed his cell and called his father. "Dad," he whispered.

By T. Styles

Banks sighed. "Hello, son."

"Dad, do you, do you remember who you bought this island from?"

"Why you asking me?"

"Pops, please."

Banks took a deep breath. "I bought it from a family who couldn't afford to upkeep the land. There was another mansion on it but it was overrun with pests and nothing like the vision I had for my family. So I tore it down and built what I wanted."

"A mansion? Like...a drug dealer's mansion?"

"Joey, is something wrong?"

"No...I..." He stood on his knees and looked at the strange man in the linen suit again, before sitting back down. "Just...just come home when you can."

"I will, son. I will."

When he ended the call, he was creeped out to see Roxana standing in the doorway. The baby of the family, at fifteen, she was holding a brown teddy bear, with her head tilted to the right...smiling awkwardly.

No doubt she scared the fuck out of him.

"What you want?" Joey asked, standing up.

"My father's coming back and soon you all will die." She laughed lightly and ran away.

Joey was perplexed. Like Banks he assumed she was mute.

He also assumed Ives was her father. So what did she mean?

What was going on?

CHAPTER TWENTY
PRESENT DAY
CHRISTMAS EVE

Banks lay in bed with a glass of scotch in hand. Over the months since losing Minnie, it had become a normal process. So much so that, he drank it exclusively, almost never drinking water.

When his cell rang, he swallowed what was in his glass and answered. "Yeah."

"It's me. Zion."

Banks sat up straight. "Is Harris okay?" He paused, hoping he wouldn't hear the worst. Bail was denied long ago and the government seemed intent on punishing him for the crime of peeking into a mailbox. And he was concerned he would lose another child. This one to the system. Still, he had no intentions on going back to Wales Island without him.

"Yeah, he's fine." He paused. "He been hard for months. Like not scared of nothing."

Banks relaxed into the bed. "Then what you want?"

"I think Linden making a move to leave or something. I overheard him in his bunk telling somebody where his money at. Maybe he made bail."

Banks frowned and sat back up. "Bail, are you sure? 'Cause I know for a fact if he was given bail he would've posted it months ago."

"I think he didn't want it paid because he was trying to get at Harris. But he been too protected so maybe he's going home."

There was no way Banks could see Linden going free. Especially since he was certain that along with Mason, he was responsible for his daughter's death. Besides, who burned her body, forcing him to have to bury a crisp corpse? The only blessing was that Bet didn't have to see her that way. He handled the funeral all-alone. He didn't even tell her parents or Spacey.

It was just him and Shay.

Then there was the part of him that knew that Linden would be seeking revenge for him murdering Mason.

When his other line beeped he looked at it and saw it was his wife. He had been ignoring most of her calls, refusing to tell her that Minnie was no longer alive, for fear that she would make things

By T. Styles

heavier for Joey. His actions were cruel, he was certain, but what could he do? In his mind it was best to tell her personally that their daughter was gone.

Then there was Spacey, who had not been back at the house since the plane landed, reducing their relationship to daily text messages. He wanted to search the world for him but he was a man, who he finally understood he couldn't force to live the way he wanted him to anymore.

So had he given up on it all?

Not even close.

"Hit Linden."

"You sure?"

"Yeah. But make sure you careful with my son on part two of the plan." He paused. "No major organs."

"Sir...you sure we should do that. I'm worried something will—"

"Do what the fuck I said!" He pointed into the air. "I want that nigga gone! Tonight!"

Mason was asleep in the bed when all of a sudden he sat up straight when he felt a *darkness* in his room. When he turned the lamp on he was surprised to see his wife. "What is it?" He leaned back into the headboard and yawned. "You found Arlyndo? He okay?"

He grabbed his cell to look at his phone. There were many missed calls and his heart rocked as he scrolled up looking at each. Normally he would sleep with the phone next to his head, but lately he had been so exhausted from searching for his youngest that he was too beat.

She moved closer. "Linden was murdered, Mason. And I'm so sorry."

He frowned. "What you talking about murdered? I just talked to my brother the other day."

"I know."

Although he was sitting down, the room felt as if it were spinning. So he sat up slowly, trying to process it all. Did he actually hear what he thought he had? "How...how did you find out?"

She took a deep breath. "Dragon." She sat on the bed and looked over at him. "He said he was stabbed by many men. They felt like it was a revenge hit or something but you can't be sure

By T. Styles

with Dragon. You can't forget that he wants to see you fall. He know about the beef with Banks. I think it's a trap. Don't let this pull you into another fight with—"

"Fuck am I hearing?" He glared at her. "You actually still talking to that nigga? Behind my back."

"He texted."

Mason walked toward the wall and realized the weight of losing his brother was too much to fight with his wife. He needed her in the moment. He backed into it and slid down. "He could feel it." He looked over at her. "Linden knew something would happen to him and that's why he wanted me to have his paper."

"I get that but this doesn't mean it was Banks," Jersey said, rushing up to him. The last thing she wanted was for him to take away the peace he had just promised. "Please don't wage war again."

She sounded like a clown in his opinion.

"Outside of my sons, Linden was the last of my blood. And if you think I'ma let the nigga Banks ride for this shit. You don't know me. At all."

FCI LOW – DORM
EARLIER THAT NIGHT

After Linden breathed his last breath on the floor, Kirk looked amongst all of the men who were so glued onto his every word, they couldn't catch their breaths they were so enthralled. A natural storyteller, they were sad to see the tale he just told come to an end. By now, as they glanced down at Linden it had become painfully obvious that he had succumbed to the group stabbing from earlier that evening.

It was time to kill again.

"So what you gonna do now?" Byrd asked Kirk. "Cause you may have been a boss on the street, but in here you just another nigga." He rubbed his crusty hands together. "And we not taking the rap for you for killing this dude."

"Exactly," Clay said. "You want us to stay quiet 'bout this here," He pointed at Linden, "Then you gotta grease palms."

By T. Styles

"Watch out, young niggas," Tops said standing up from the bunk. "You still talking to a king."

Suddenly Kirk's men, dispatched by Banks, moved in on the group of men who had gathered around to hear Kirk's story. There could be no witnesses. So, the soldiers slammed calloused palms down over the men's lips as they were jabbed multiple times in the back. By the time the carnage was over, eight trained killers with dripping blood-covered shanks in their hands, surrounded Tops, Byrd and Clay.

The only surviving three.

"So you gonna kill us too?" Tops said. "I could've blew up your spot the moment we got locked up together," he paused. "Especially since you lied that we helped you break into that mailbox." He pointed at him. "But I didn't."

Kirk smiled. "I lied on you for a reason."

"And what's that?" He asked through clenched teeth.

"To kill you." He paused. "For starting this war. I saw you fire in our window. At first I wasn't sure who you were but now I know you were with the Lou's. And I don't want you around me or my family."

Byrd and Clay looked behind them at the men, but realized they couldn't run. Instead they were grabbed...two killers on Clay and Byrd and Four on Tops.

"Come on, man," Byrd begged. "Don't hurt me."

"Yeah, Kirk, you ain't gotta do this," Clay added.

"Before I told my story I asked if you were sure you wanted to hear the rest. Each of you said yes. Now you know the reason for my question."

Byrd was shanked quickly and lost his fight. Clay soon followed and entered the afterlife. Tops gave a good try, but in the end his enormous body hit the floor like the rest, as blood gushed from his wounds.

Standing amongst dead inmates, Kirk took a deep breath and looked at his men.

"Why you hit Linden early?" Kirk asked Zion. "I paid for next week."

"You ain't hear?" He responded. "Linden was getting out on bail tomorrow."

"Nah, I ain't know 'bout that." Kirk smiled. "Good looking out though."

Zion grinned. "No doubt."

"You know what you have to do now." Kirk paused. "No major organs." He raised his arms.

194   *By T. Styles*

Zion looked at the men behind him and back at Kirk. They all shook their heads no, wanting no part of the gruesome chore.

"You sure about this, man?" He paused. "I don't want Banks mad at me."

"This his idea," he paused. "It's part of the plan." He continued. "Now hit me."

Pulling out a fresh shank, within seconds Kirk lie on the floor, amongst the others, bleeding from the gut. In more pain than he thought was possible he whispered, "Go sound the alarm." He paused. "Quick!"

Within fifteen minutes the ambulance exceeded speed limits as it rushed away from the prison.

At that rate it was obvious Harris Kirk Wales would die from an accident, instead of the stab wound he took to the gut if they weren't careful. But the possibility of his passing put all of the passengers on edge. If he died, if he breathed his last breath, they were certain they would follow behind him soon enough.

And they were right.

As Kirk lied in a bed of his own blood, eyes on the ceiling, the frantic look of two paramedics above him, he thought about his life...

It was supposed to be simple.

Now he realized, nothing ever was.

Banks, Shay and a few of his men stood in the hospital lobby area. They were waiting on word of Harris' injury. The plan was originally to hijack the ambulance after Harris was stabbed. Next they would transfer him to the location where a doctor waiting could save his life. Once stable, he would be flown to Wales Island.

But after getting word that the injuries were too severe, he let the ambulance go unstopped. In the hopes that he would receive better care.

All he wanted now was his son to make it out of this failed attempt to escape alive.

"Banks," a teenager yelled from the lobby. "Is that you?"

Banks' men immediately surrounded the youngster, due to not feeling his energy. Had he known Banks closely, he would've realized that his son was in the ICU. And so his spirit would've been kinder and not so aggressive.

He was definitely an antagonist.

196   *By T. Styles*

"Back the fuck up!" Rev said with a shove to the young man's chest.

The kid smiled. "Come on, man." He tried to step closer and Rev grabbed him by his coat. "All I wanna ask is if it's true?"

Banks frowned. "Fuck is you talking about?"

"Are you really a bitch?" He laughed. "I mean, do you got a pussy?"

The comment stung so hard that it temporarily shocked Banks and his crew, leaving them all speechless. Banks never had to deal with his sexuality before, because nobody knew before Mason dropped the ball.

It was Rev who regained his composure, quickly and so he stole him in the mouth. Causing two of his teeth to spin out on the floor like dice.

A few seconds later, he was escorted, kicked, punched and pinched all the way out the door.

When the boy was gone, Rev walked up to Banks. "Sorry about that, sir. I didn't—"

"I ain't worried about nothing but my son right now!" Banks yelled, embarrassed beyond belief. "Now step the fuck up out my face." Banks looked around to see who else was studying the way he moved.

Everyone was.

Strangers.

Rev.

And even his men.

He felt so ashamed he got dizzy and sat down. He would never forgive Mason in death for his betrayal. Ever.

After thirty more minutes, the doctor approached with a serious look on his face.

Banks moped into his house slowly.

Each step erect, as if he were a robot. He temporarily lost the ability to hear after the doctor told him that Harris Kirk Wales had died. It was a tiny blessing that he couldn't perceive sound in the moment, because Shay followed him, with a piercing cry so heart wrenching he would've fell to his knees.

To some, at first, Banks appeared cold after learning about his son's fate. Even when the doctor said that Harris didn't make it, he didn't bat an eye. Instead he walked outside, got in his

By T. Styles

truck and pulled off calmly from the hospital. He was so numb that he didn't know that upon receiving the news, that Shay had never left his side.

But there he was.

Inside the walls of the Wales Mansion, where ironically it's emptiness echoed what he felt in his soul. He was made aware that the Wales family had been diminished yet again.

Walking into the office, he closed the door softly. It was at that moment that the weight of what happened occurred to him like a blow to the face. His body gave way to gravity and forced him to his knees. His voice felt strained as he opened his mouth and nothing came out.

But when he regained the use of vocalization he screamed loudly. It was the same painful cry exacerbated more by the fact that in less than six months, he had lost two children.

One on Christmas Day.

Zion knew his day was coming.

He had already given the money from his books to his daughter, divided the commissary up between his most loyal comrades and waited for death day. He didn't know whom Banks would send to murder him for killing Harris, but he knew somebody would come when he least expected it.

To his surprise, Banks had solicited Zion's closest friends. The same ones who took his gifts earlier in the day, despite knowing they would later act as hired killers in an effort to take his life. This made the pain worse, which he was certain, was Banks' plan.

As he sat on the edge of his bed, he stood up when he saw the two men enter. Trying to save face, he smiled. "Wow...just like this, huh?"

"He died," Inmate number 235679 said shrugging. "And you did that." He pointed at him with a prison made shank.

Zion nodded. "So when did Banks pay you?"

"Does it matter?" He paused, as both of them leaped, poked and chopped him eighteen bloody times, the same age Harris was when he died.

Twenty-two minutes later, Banks was sitting in his office when the text message showing

By T. Styles

Zion's decapitated head on his phone. He had already given the order for the paramedics who were driving Harris to be murdered, and it was confirmed earlier that afternoon. Now that Zion was gone, he received partial relief, although it was not nearly enough to soothe his pain.

Besides...nothing could bring back Harris Kirk Wales.

"Rest in peace, son," Banks said. "Rest in peace."

CHAPTER TWENTY-ONE

Bet lay face up on the beach as the sun beamed down on her body. And it was obvious that although it was one of the hottest days on Wales Island, she was too out of her mind to notice. After barely eating for months on end, her flesh almost appeared as if it were falling off her body and could no longer support her frame.

"Ma," Joey said walking out on the beach and sitting next to her. "What you doing? You been out here too long."

She looked at him and smiled. "You remind me of him you know?"

He took a deep breath, trying his best to be strong. But seeing her in the way she had been lately, spoiled the enjoyment of the island for him all together. No longer was he interested in sex with the Nunez sisters. It was all he could do to keep his mind off of his mother, to make sure she was okay. As well as pay close attention to the Nunez's and their strange motives.

"Who I remind you of, ma?"

By T. Styles

She smiled. "You know." She sat up and touched the side of his face. "I can tell in your eyes you know who I'm talking about."

He knew she was referring to Banks but since he wasn't his real father, he felt she was yet again losing her mind. The only likeness they had was the fact that they were all light-skinned. "Ma...please." He gripped her hand. "Let me warm you up some food. You gonna die if—"

"Something's wrong back home." She sat up and looked over at him. "And I can't eat until I know for sure what it is." Her eyes widened and her focus fell on the beach, although she wasn't really looking at it. "I need to know that the darkness in my head is all made up. That it's all a lie."

"Nothing's wrong, ma." He pulled her into an unwanted hug. "I talked to Harris yesterday and he fine. Plus you know Minnie with Arlyndo somewhere. Pops gonna find her and he gonna get Harris. Try not to worry."

"Nah. Something's off, honey. And until I get the magic words...until I get the code that only God knows I need to hear, I'm not going to eat a thing."

Banks hadn't showered in five days. Shay who was barely functional herself, dampened washcloths to wipe his face while he was asleep but that was the extent of his bathing. Instead of taking care of himself, he drank more liquor like water, and ate whatever didn't need a lot of preparation for food.

All while he continued to fall deeper into despair.

When the front door opened, Rev walked inside. It wasn't until that time that Banks realized it was even unlocked, mainly because he didn't care.

Moving toward the living room, Rev was shocked at the horrible condition he found Banks in and yet he understood. His beard had gotten so long and out of control, it touched his clavicle. He was soiled and ashy. Nothing like the boss he was accustomed to.

But again Rev understood. He would never be able to endure one child dying, let alone two.

By T. Styles

"Rev," Shay said softly, walking up behind him. Rev turned around and faced her. Although she looked bad, she was holding up better than the boss. "Did you want anything to drink?" She asked softly, a hard cry ready to reveal itself if he said anything loving. Losing Harris set her back in ways she never thought were possible.

He placed a soft hand on her shoulder. "I'm fine, Shay." He paused. "Leave us, sweetheart. I have to talk to Banks alone." He hugged her.

When she walked away, Rev approached the couch and looked down at Banks. "What you doing, sir?" He asked softly. "I don't know what you going through, but you can't give up. You can't end shit like this."

Banks looked up at him. "Just...just get out."

"I can't do that."

Banks shook his head in irritation.

Rev took a deep breath and sat next to him. "I never thought I would be in this drug shit forever. Before I met you and your father, I had so much going on in my life on the bad side that I was sure I wasn't going to make it. My kid had cancer. My wife left me for my uncle and I was just...devastated. So I made a pact. I said, 'God, if *you give me a sign that you need me...just one...I won't take this gun and put a bullet in my head.'"*

Banks took a deep breath and gave him his undivided attention. Because although Banks didn't want to have the worst thoughts, he too entertained suicide after losing two kids.

"I got a sign," Rev said. "And you know what the sign was?"

Silence.

"You came into my life. The son of the woman my father killed years earlier." He paused. "And you and your father needed my help to build. And I knew I could help you."

Banks rotated his head toward him quickly. "What you...what you just say to me?"

"My father killed your mother at the liquor store that night."

Banks glared.

"When your father approached me to help the business, I recognized your face from the news that night," Rev continued. "The only thing I couldn't understand at first was why the news said Angie had a daughter, when you were a...a man."

"I want you out my fucking house." Banks said through clenched teeth.

By T. *Styles*

"I know you hate me. But I told you the truth because I love you. And it's not just about business. I really look at my job being to protect you. So at the risk of you never wanting to see me again, I wanted no more secrets between us."

"Get out my house, Rev. I promise I won't ask again."

"Okay...okay I'll go." Rev sighed placing two palms in the air. "Before I leave, I wanted you to know that Mason is alive. And if you want to survive, if you have anything else to live for, you have to get out of this house now."

Banks leaped up.

Rev rose too.

A strange sensation over came Banks upon hearing the news. It was a mixture of fear, confusion and happiness, which made him feel sick.

How could it be true?

"What are you—"

"You have to leave, Banks. And you have to leave now."

After learning of Harris's death, Mason gave Banks the honor of allowing him to bury his son. But that small mercy would be the extent of his graciousness.

It was judgment night.

He was in a caravan that included six others and they were driving through the night, each man on the way to pay Banks Wales a visit. It was obvious to Mason after the hit on Linden, that Banks was trying to snuff out the entire Louisville family, and he wasn't about to let his actions ride.

Besides, who would be next? One of his sons? Nah.

He wasn't worried about moving to the island anymore. Mason's motivation was clearly revenge. Nothing more and nothing less. Banks Wales, his best friend, must die.

He was a half a mile from the property when sirens blasted through the night air. "Boss...it's the cops," JD said to Mason, while looking out the rearview mirror.

Mason glared "I see that, nigga." He looked behind him and back at JD. "What, you got a taillight out or something?"

By T. Styles

"No...at least I don't think. So...what you want me to do?"

"Tuck the guns." He paused. "And pull over. Tell the others to fan out too. Ain't no need in all of us getting caught up."

JD quickly obeyed and alerted the others before bringing the car to a stop. Within seconds an officer approached the driver side. "License and registration."

The moment Mason heard the man's voice, he recognized it implicitly. "What up, Mason?"

He glared.

He felt so stupid.

Jersey was right.

It was a trap.

"So you told my wife about Linden getting murdered and waited, because you knew what I would do next?"

Dragon smiled. "You're a creature of habit. That will always be your downfall."

For now the murder of Banks Wales would have to wait.

CHAPTER TWENTY-TWO

B lakeslee and Mason were walking out the building on the way to the store. She allowed him to put his arm around her, not because she liked it, but mainly because Mason made promises that so far he maintained.

For instance, in secret, he allowed her to wear his clothes whenever she went over his house. He allowed her to pretend like they were both boys, when no one was looking. She would play for hours in the mirror wearing his hats and learning to walk and talk like Mason Louisville.

In the beginning Mason thought it was cute but after awhile, he started to suspect that maybe Blakeslee was being a bit more serious about role-play time than he understood. It soon became obvious that she wasn't pretending to be a boy. She was pretending to be a girl and he prayed in his heart that this ungodly phase would pass.

It hadn't.

They just exited their building when they saw a pretty little girl sitting on the step. She was crying and looked sad and although Mason could care

By T. *Styles*

less about the young female and her tears, Blakeslee was in awe of her beauty.

Crawling from up under Mason's hold, she quickly sat next to her. "What's...what's wrong?" Blakeslee asked.

The girl wiped her tears. "My daddy left to go to the store last night. And he ain't come back yet."

"Let's go, Blakeslee," Mason yelled, wanting her attention all to himself.

"You scared something mighta happened to him?" Blakeslee asked, ignoring him.

Defeated, Mason sat next to Blakeslee.

"Yeah...I mean...he do stuff like this sometimes." She sniffled. "But never overnight."

"Where your mama?"

"She gone." She said softly. "That's all I wanna say about that right now."

Blakeslee nodded and extended her hand. "My name's Blakeslee. What's yours?"

"Nikki." She shook her hand.

"Nikki...I like that." Blakeslee blushed.

From that moment on Nikki, Blakeslee and Mason were an item. For two years they grew closer and closer in their bond. And where you saw one you saw the trio. Mason had even abandoned all of his friends for the sake of the girls but with time, it became obvious that Blakeslee and Nikki had a relationship that extended deeper than the one he had with his girl. And so after awhile, he began to feel like a third wheel and he hated Nikki for it.

Secretly he dreamed of a day when Nikki would die a terrible death, although that day would not come until much later. Instead he was forced to sit with his emotions, knowing that if he gave Blakeslee an ultimatum, by saying it was either she or he, that Blakeslee would choose Nikki in a heartbeat.

One day Mason had convinced his babysitter to let him spend the night over Blakeslee's house. Mason's father was never in the picture around this time, electing instead to dedicate his life for the sake of money. And so he always charged young girls in the neighborhood and his brother to watch his son. The problem was plentiful. The girls Mason's father paid didn't care what he did and so in secret his uncle took to molesting him.

Mason grew tired of finding new ways to keep his uncle off of his body, and so he retreated to Blakeslee's home for safety.

On this particular night, Mason had gone over Blakeslee's early, only to find out that Dennis had

By T. *Styles*

been locked up for a small crime earlier that day. Blakeslee's mother was beside herself with grief, and didn't seem to notice what was happening around her. What was she going to do without her protector? Her husband? Her lover?

When Mason walked into the front door, Angie walked up to him and gripped him up in her arms. Her tears washed against his cheeks and his body was rigid not knowing what to say to appease her.

"I'm okay, I'm okay," she said as if anyone asked. She finally released him. "The kids are in the room." She stepped back and crossed her arms over her chest. "Did you bring your clothes? For the sleepover?"

He nodded yes.

She sniffled and wiped her nose with the back of her hand. "I'll...I'll order some pizza later."

He smiled and ran to the back of the room quickly. Not only to get away from her but to see his girl. It was his life's mission to never allow them to have more time together alone than what was required.

Excited to see her face, he dropped his bag in the hallway.

Before he opened the door, he heard a noise that he couldn't put into words directly. All he knew was that it sounded passionate and excitable at the same time. Curious, slowly he opened the door and saw Blakeslee and Nikki sitting on the bed, kissing one another. It appeared to be a soft kiss but Blakeslee seemed transformed by each passing second.

Hurt in ways he didn't know was possible, he backed out without being seen by the two betrayers. Walking slowly in the kitchen, he was barely able to remain standing. Blakeslee wasn't just something to do for the hustler's son. She was his existence and he knew that no matter what, even despite seeing the two together, that they would always remain connected in their later lives.

Carefully he walked up to Angie. She was removing and replacing dishes from cabinet to cabinet with no apparent purpose. He cleared his throat and said. "Um...Mrs. Wales."

She didn't hear him.

He stepped further inside. "Mrs. Wales."

Clutching a cast iron pan, she stopped in mid motion. "Yes?" Her eyes were glassed over and although she was there, it was obvious that her mind was someplace else. "What is it, honey?"

He pointed behind him. "You have to go...you gotta go to the room."

By T. *Styles*

"Is everything okay?" She frowned, placing the pan on the counter.

"You have to see." He paused. "For yourself."

Slowly she walked to the room and opened the door with Mason following. When she saw Blakeslee and Nikki engaged in such an erotic act for their age, she snatched Nikki and dragged her toward the front door by her hair.

"What are you doing to my daughter?!" She yelled at the child. "What a little slut you are! What a little freak you are!"

When the door was ajar, she tossed the little girl out like trash in the hallway and slammed and locked the door behind herself.

With wild fists, Blakeslee swung and attacked her mother in an effort to follow Nikki, but Angie plastered herself on the door like paste. She took each painful blow from her only child, but nothing Blakeslee did seemed to work.

Angie wouldn't budge.

Mason, on the other hand was stunned at how hurt his girlfriend seemed to be.

He felt responsible after seeing Blakeslee cry hysterically and strike her mother as if she were a stranger. It pulled out his heart as he realized that *despite being young, that he had hurt the love of his life beyond repair.*

"Let me leave!" Blakeslee yelled kicking and screaming. "Let me leave! I hate you! I fucking hate you!"

Her words stung her already fragile mother.

And so she backed away, allowing Blakeslee to pull the door open and run out into the night. Without Dennis' strength, she wasn't fit to handle herself, let alone a distraught child.

For twenty-four hours nobody knew where Blakeslee was as they scoured Baltimore trying to find her. Nikki's aunt had taken Nikki into her home later and it just so happened that she too lived in the same building. Nikki told the police repeatedly that she had no knowledge of Blakeslee's whereabouts but no one seemed to believe her.

It wasn't until the next day that a jogger, on a local bridge, overlooking a small body of water, heard an agonizing cry. When he looked below he was shocked to see Blakeslee lying on a bank of rocks, blood pouring out of her body.

Some hours later, in the hospital room, Angie walked inside slowly to see Blakeslee. She looked at her only child, who was covered from head to

By T. Styles

toe in a body cast. She had fractured her back and broken her leg. "Why, baby?" She sniffled. "Why would you...why would you try to hurt yourself?"

Blakeslee was so grief stricken, she could barely form the words to say what had been ripping her up since she could remember. "I don't know."

Angie wiped her hair behind her ear. That wasn't going to be good enough. "Talk to me. You...you have to know why."

It seemed like forever, but finally she mouthed the words, "I hate me and I wanna die!"

From that moment on Angie was forced to deal with what she already knew. Of course she acted brashly upon seeing her daughter kiss another little girl. But her real anger came from one fact. That despite her own madness, she always knew her little girl was suffering with her identity and she hated herself for not addressing it sooner. In a sense, some would later say, that Angie's mental illness was directly related to her daughter's pain.

In the beginning, to her and Dennis, Mason was the answer to Blakeslee's problem. He was a cute little boy who was enamored with their daughter so surely, with time, their child would come to see this and like him back.

Why couldn't Blakeslee see her beauty and sex as a blessing instead of a curse?

Still, there was work to do and she knew where to go.

The following day, Angie went to visit Dennis in jail.

"She's gonna have to change schools," he said, upon hearing the news about the lengths his daughter went to, to be with another girl. "She can't be no lesbian. I'm not gonna be able to deal with that shit." He pointed at her. "Lesbians and faggies go against everything God stands for." He pointed at her from behind plexi-glass, having just robbed a few niggas for wealth. "So if she gonna be with other bitches, she has to live the right way."

"What are you saying?"

"She has to be what she sees herself as." He shrugged. "My daughter died the day she jumped off that bridge. If she wants this life, if she wants this world, she will be my son."

Angie moved uneasily in her seat. In her mind this was far from what they should be doing, but being unstable mentally herself, she couldn't think of a better plan. "I don't know about that." She hugged herself.

By T. Styles

"You don't gotta know. I'm telling you how it's going down."

"So what kind of name would we give her?" Angie said, still vastly confused at what he was saying.

"You can't be with me if you think I robbed them banks!" An inmate on the right of him yelled who was on the visit with a woman. "You might as well go back to wherever you came from talking that dumb shit." He jumped up and left the cubicle, leaving a woman who came to visit him alone.

Slowly Dennis looked at Angie. "Banks. His name will be Banks Wales."

CHAPTER TWENTY-THREE

Bet was in the kitchen slicing onions. After days without eating, suddenly she awakened extremely hungry. Joey was so satisfied with the hopes that maybe she was finally well, that he sat and watched her in the kitchen as she prepared seafood gumbo like he was a child. "Ma, what happened?" He paused. "You feel better now?"

"What you talking about what happened?" She dropped the vegetables in the pot with the seafood that was steaming.

"You said until you heard the magic words you wouldn't eat. So what—"

"Haven't heard them yet." She shrugged. "Don't know if I will."

He frowned and adjusted in the kitchen chair. "So what—"

"Joey, I'm hungry and I'm alive. Not everything goes in an organized pattern. Be happy that—"

"I got it."

She smiled. "Do you?"

He nodded yes. Actually he had no idea why her mood flip-flopped the way it did but he was pleased that at least she was up at the moment.

220   *By T. Styles*

He didn't want to antagonize her and make things worse. And instead of asking her a million questions, he simply made it his responsibility to watch her.

But it was obvious she was still weak. Because while slicing green peppers, she almost fell over on the kitchen floor. Concerned, Joey jumped to help but she raised her hand for him to stop.

Slowly she walked over to the table and sat down with the knife and vegetables in hand.

Seconds later, Oswalda walked in and looked at Bet. Always the creepy little one, Roxana strolled in behind her and sat on the floor by the fridge, stroking her teddy bear.

Instead of being happy, Oswalda seemed disappointed she was cooking instead of suffering.

"You're up," Oswalda said.

Joey looked at the two sisters and frowned. He couldn't stand either one of them but it was Oswalda that he hated most. "Why you looking all crazy and shit?" He asked Oswalda. "She better. Be glad you and your family don't have to cook tonight. Although it ain't like you been cooking around here anyway. "

She shrugged. "We don't mind preparing meals." She observed Bet again. "At least I don't."

He stood up and walked toward the exit. "I bet you don't mind." He walked out and Oswalda followed him into the hallway.

"Listen, I know you don't like me but I gotta say something."

"What?"

"I spend a lot of time with her. And I know it may seem like she's on the mend but don't get too excited. I've seen this type of thing before and she can always relapse. Just enjoy the time you have with her while she's in her right state of mind."

"Why would you say some shit like that to me?"

"I was just trying to—"

"Go take care of Mrs. Wales." Tobias said walking up behind Joey.

"I was just—"

"Oswalda, go!" He yelled at his sister.

She rolled her eyes and stormed down the hallway.

"Wanna bowl?" Tobias asked. "Or do you keep your game play for my sisters only?"

"I haven't talked to Cassandra or Emetine since...well...you know."

"We bowling or not?"

Five minutes later they were in the alley. "So what's the deal with Oswalda? And your family?" Joey asked holding a shimmering black bowling ball while positioning his arm. He aimed and released, knocking down four pens.

"She not my sister. And my family, well, we can be suspicious of people sometimes."

"But this is our house," Joey frowned and sat in the chair in the alley. "So what the fuck you talking about?"

Tobias walked over to the bar. "You want a beer or—"

"Come sit the fuck down and tell me what you mean. And tell me why everybody acting so creepy all of a sudden."

Tobias took a deep breath and walked over to one of the two luxury recliners. "As far as Oswalda, if I had to sum it up, I'd say my mother has a problem with strays."

"Nigga, I'ma need you to do more explaining than that."

"At first it was animals and then it was...well...Oswalda's parents were killed by militia. Instead of joining the cause like my mother and father, they were trying to hide.

Before long the militia caught up with them and they murdered her parents in front of her. Oswalda was about five years old. So when my parents found her, she had been living off whatever she could eat, even the flesh of her parents, which was rotted so badly she got sick. And almost died."

Joey sat back. His heart rocked due to what he was hearing. "What the fuck." He whispered.

"Yeah...I know...it's hard for most people to believe but its true. Anyway, I'm not about guessing, but I believe it was one of the reasons she is the way she is. You know?"

"I do now." He paused. "So what about Roxana? She said something about her father coming."

Tobias' eyes grew bigger. "No she didn't. She can't talk."

Joey glared and just like that, everything Tobias told him a few seconds ago he knew to be a lie. Besides, he heard the creepy girl speak himself. "Yeah...maybe it was just me."

"So...you gonna tell your pops?"

Joey sighed and wiped his hand down his face. "Nah, he got enough on his plate right now."

"Thank you, man."

"Don't thank me," Joey pointed at him. "Just chill out with toting guns in the house and tell Oswalda to fall back. I'm taking care of my mother now."

"You won't hear an argument from me."

CHAPTER TWENTY-FOUR

It was completely dark as rain pounded against the window in Banks' bedroom. He was drunk out of his mind and had fallen into a deeper haze. Shay had gone to visit a friend and surprisingly with her gone, he felt the sting of what his life had come to even more.

Harris and Minnie were dead.

Mason was possibly alive.

His world was a bag of trash and the only progress he managed since Harris' death was that he showered an hour before, but it did nothing for his mood.

He was about to drink more vodka when the bedroom door opened. Standing in the doorway, was a silhouette he recognized although he thought he was seeing things. Was he that drunk? And then she spoke.

"Wow, the beard is different."

Silence.

"So you gonna just lay there and die?" Nidia continued, after not receiving a response.

Banks sat the vodka bottle on the table by the bed.

226 *By T. Styles*

He was preparing to cut on the lamp when she said, "Leave it off. The last thing I want is to see you like this."

He sat up and she sat on the edge of the bed. "What you doing here, Nidia? Why you in my house?"

"Are you asking if I came to kill you? Because you left the doors to your home open." She shrugged. "If you ask me it looks like you're hoping somebody will put a bullet in your head."

"I'm good."

"I'm disappointed." She sighed. "Had plans for you but if you're going to kill yourself, well...basically you're doing the work for me and that's not fair."

"Why are you here?"

She sighed. "I heard about your son and daughter. And since you made a big deal about getting out of the game for your family, I figured you must be devastated if you are giving up so easily."

"I don't need your pity."

"You need something, Banks." She kicked off her Prada shoes and crawled in bed next to him. He moved back a little. "It's okay to be...vulnerable sometimes." She touched the side of his face. "When you've been strong for most of your life. I don't consider that weak at all."

He took a deep breath. "I'm not weak."

"Never said you were, Banks."

"But you're thinking it. I can tell by the sound of your voice."

"If you could see my eyes you would know that weak is the furthest thing from my mind when it comes to you."

"You wanted me to keep the lights out," he sighed, bored with it all. "Remember?"

She giggled and took a deep breath. "Banks, you asked me why I'm here and I don't have a good answer for that. Except that when I didn't see you making moves on the street, I grew worried."

"So you following me now?"

"Yes."

He wiped his hand down his face. "I can't give you what you want, Nidia. We've been here before."

She moved closer. "How do you know when you haven't even tried?" She crawled on top of him. He couldn't see her face, just shadows, but in the darkness her youth shined, and for some odd reason, he felt like humoring one of his worst enemies sexually.

Banks wanted to be real again. "I'm not a—"

"Man...," she said completing his sentence. "I remember but I don't care." She lowered her head and kissed his lips.

Her kiss tasted of mint and desperation and that too was pleasing to Banks. So he wrapped his arms around her waist, lifted her up and laid on top of her. Looking down into her eyes he removed his thickness from his pants and tore off her panties before entering her body.

She was so surprised at how quickly her mind tricked her, that she had an out of body experience. She knew he was female and yet his strength, his smell, and even the way he appeared to lust after her in the moment, caused her to buy into whom Banks believed himself to be.

A warm-blooded man.

Slowly he moved in and out of her body. Within seconds he pumped harder when he heard the rhythmic sounds of her moans. "Banks...you...you feel so good. How did you...how are you doing that?"

Compliments were not necessary. This was sexual and it would be over the moment he was satisfied, whether she liked it or not. And so after ten more minutes, he had officially fucked The Plug.

It wasn't romantic.

It was more animalistic.

And when the job was done, he fell into a deep sleep.

The next morning he had awoken, only to see her staring at him with a smile on her face. "I understand now."

He sat up slowly and leaned against the headboard, running his fingers through his beard, down his cheeks. "Understand what, Nidia?"

She sat up and smiled brighter. "Why I was so attracted to you. Why women look at you like a...I mean—"

"You have to leave." He paused. "And I mean like right now."

She frowned. "Why? You've obviously made a decision that you don't want to be a family man anymore." She paused. "That...that you want to stay in Baltimore and—"

"You don't know anything about me. Especially if you think I'd abandon my family and never go back to my island."

"So why haven't you?" She glared.

"The hardest thing in the world is telling someone you care about that two of your children are gone. While believing it's your fault." He paused. "Now I have to do things my way, but I will return to them, Nidia."

"But I think what we shared last night shows I can be with you." She placed her hand over her heart. "It shows that I can be with a woman and—"

"Fuck you just say?"

"What?"

"You called me a—"

"A woman?" She interrupted, not understanding the source of his rage. "And I mean, I meant no disrespect by it but I want you to know that I can accept whatever this is. Whatever you think you are. That I can learn to be a lesbian or—"

Now she made him all kinds of angry. She was so far off from who he was that it was sickening. "Nidia, get your shit and get the fuck up out my house."

Her breath rose and fell in her chest. "So you're willing to do this to me when you know what I can do to you?"

"I'm not gonna tell you again."

She was so humiliated it felt to her as if the room was spinning. "Jameson!" She yelled, her jaw twitching. "Come in here right now!"

Upon hearing her call someone else's name, Banks leapt out of bed quickly. Although he never knew her to roll in the streets alone, he didn't stop to think that someone else was in his house. After all, they had slept together and he was drunk out of his mind before falling into a sex-alcohol induced sleep. But his ignorance would not free him from danger.

Within seconds a medium height stout man opened the bedroom door. And just that quickly, he was aiming a weapon in Banks' direction.

Seeing Banks' fear, she smiled. "You wanna say to me what you said earlier, Banks?"

Banks swallowed the lump in his throat. "Listen, I don't have time to do this with you now, Nidia." He said, with two palms facing her direction. The only thing he could think about was Joey, Spacey and his wife. "Maybe we can talk about this later." He looked at the stranger.

"Alone." The odd part is prior to this going on, Banks didn't care if he lived or died. But suddenly he had a desire to survive.

"Banks, you're coming with me," Nidia said plainly. "I really am sorry. I'll let you call your family later."

He glared. "Nidia, I can't go anywhere with you. I have to get back to my family and—"

"Maybe I'm giving you the impression that you're—"

"Argggghhh!" Jameson cried out suddenly.

When Banks and Nidia focused on him, they saw Shay holding a bloody knife, which she plunged into Jameson's neckline once and then a second time. "I'm sorry, Banks," Shay said shivering. "I thought he was going to hurt you. And I didn't want to...to be by myself again." The child trembled as she looked down at the dying man on the floor.

Wanting to seize the moment, Banks leaped over the bed, grabbed the knife from her hand and hugged Shay with one arm. "Oh, my God, thank you! Thank you so much!" He said kissing the top of her head many times. "You can leave now, Shay."

"Are you s...sure?" She shivered.

"I got it."

Shay nodded and ran away.

Now under control he asked, "Tell me right now why I should let you go," Banks said, walking up to Nidia with a bloodied knife.

"Please don't hurt me," she said with raised hands.

"You not answering my question."

She swallowed. "People know I'm here, Banks. And if you have anybody in the country that you care about, or your wife cares about, the last person you want to hurt is me. Be smart. You know what I'm saying is true."

CHAPTER TWENTY-FIVE

Mason sat on the bunk in his cell.

He knew something was coming, although he couldn't say what. Since the day he had been brought inside, other inmates looked as if they had ideas for his life. Ideas that involved hurting him in some way, although he couldn't be sure why. All he wanted was to get out and get his family to safety. Because *on everything* he was certain that Dragon was trying to do all he could to separate him from his wife, so he could have her to himself.

He was also positive that the bond that Dragon and his wife shared when they were children went deeper than she let on originally. And if they were going to survive after this, he would demand that she tell him the truth.

After speaking to his lawyer again, who stated he didn't have a bail hearing set, despite it being the law, for now he would have to sit patiently and wait for Dragon's next move.

"I want another phone call!" Mason yelled through the bars, although he was certain the guards would ignore him as usual.

To his surprise within a few seconds a guard approached the cells and unlocked the door. "You gonna stay in or not, Louisville?"

Mason was stunned so he didn't move right away. "Yeah...I...I gotta make a call."

"Let's go then, inmate!" He frowned. "Before I change my mind."

Mason walked out suspiciously, while looking back at the guard who was following him. When he made it to the phone he called the one man his brother warned him never to call again. Besides, he had yet to repay the debt he owed for the man's part in killing Banks' pilot friend, so adding onto the debt when he didn't know the price was dangerous.

Still, the moment he made it to the phone, he called Whoyawanmetabe.

"It's Mason. I need your help again," he said.

After giving Whoyawanmetabe the run down in a deep whisper, he finally felt as if something would move in his name. So he made another call to his oldest son.

"I can't talk long, so let me be quick."

"Okay, Pops. What's going on? Where you at?"

"Dragon got me locked up." He paused. "Where your mother?"

By T. Styles

"Dragon came by last night...he took her when I was sleep." He paused. "Howard and Patterson tried to fight but nothing worked."

"Fuck!" Mason said, dragging his hand down his face. "Listen, I need you and your brothers to go get her, Derrick. Before he hurts her."

"We'll try, Pops...was waiting on your word. But what's going on with you? Are they gonna keep you in—"

"I don't know about all that yet. I just need you to get her out of that house. By any means."

After ending the call with Derrick, he called Jersey hoping she would answer the phone while being certain Dragon wouldn't allow her to. She did and his heart rocked the moment he heard her voice. "Baby, what the fuck is going on? Are you with Dragon?" He clenched the handset so hard it crackled.

"I...I don't know why he...he...he took me from the house and...I mean, should I call the cops?" She cried. "I thought about doing it but I know you're there and I'm so scared about what he'll do."

"No!" Mason yelled. "This nigga got the cops under his thumb." He looked back at the guard who didn't appear to be listening, although he didn't trust that it wasn't a ploy to let him use the phone, to find out his next move. "I'm sending the boys."

"Please don't," she cried. "I don't want them hurt."

"They'll be fine," Mason said harshly. "They my kids and I raised them tough."

"But—"

"There's nothing you can say to get me to change my mind." He paused. "Now do you have my shovel and seeds? Because I looked for them last night and they were gone." He was referring to his gun and bullets and although he had plenty, he secretly hoped she had them for protection.

"No."

"Maybe the boys plan on planting," he sighed. "Have you heard from Arlyndo?"

"No," she whispered. Her voice shaky and agitated. "No...nothing at all."

"Fuck!" He yelled causing the guard to focus on him. "Listen, Jersey, we have to find Arlyndo. Now I know you can't do much but if you can make some calls from where you are that will help. Because once I get out of here, I have a feeling that we'll have to go on the run."

238 *By T. Styles*

"You got one more minute, inmate," the guard said.

Mason nodded at him and focused back on the call. "Just let the boys help. I'll be out when I can. I love you."

After the call was over he went back to his cell and went to sleep. He was so exhausted, and stressed that he couldn't help his family, that he drifted off immediately.

When the cell door opened again, he shot up on his bunk. It was the same guard who walked him to the phone earlier. Except now he was waiting with a sly look on his face. It was a look that said he knew something that Mason didn't, and this immediately made him uneasy. "Come with me, inmate."

"Where we going?" Mason yawned.

Silence.

Taking the man's lack of words as serious, he followed the guard. Instead of going to the common areas, he took him on a journey to the underbellies of the jail.

"Keep walking," the guard said, directing Mason from behind.

And so they continued to walk downstairs, and into a room that looked as if it were set up for a wrestling match. Several black mats were on the center of the floor and the smell was thick, resembling a gym that had never been cleaned.

Inside of the room were four other guards who were standing across from the door. Their uniformed shirts were opened and they looked menacing.

To the left and right of the room were other inmates and they all wore sly smiles on their faces. He figured they were the audience.

"What's this?" He asked the guard who walked him inside.

"I hope you can fight." The guard locked the door and shoved Mason further in. Next the guard joined the other guards across the room.

Standing on the mat, Mason smiled, although he was horrified. "So ya'll want me to fight an inmate?" He smirked punching his fist into his palm, as if he didn't prefer to use a gun instead of his hands. "That's what this about?"

One of the guards stepped forward. "Nah, you gonna fight me." He tossed off his shirt and cracked his knuckles.

In that moment everything made sense.

Dragon's reach had touched him inside of jail, and it was certain that the plan was that he was

240   By T. Styles

not to make it out alive. Still, he had to fight. So he took off his shirt and stepped up to him. "Let's go."

The moment his arms dropped, the guard knocked him down with a tight closed fist to the mouth. "That's for you dropping, Dragon that day, inmate!"

Mason got up quickly but was hit again in the right jaw by a powerful blow. Several more whops followed and it was apparent that although Mason was a killer, boxing was a different thing all together.

It was easy to understand why he didn't possess this talent.

In the land Mason was born, you used weapons and reserved your fingers for counting paper and fucking beautiful women. What a big mistake. One if he made it out alive, he would remedy quickly.

Mason tried to regain his footing, but nothing he did gave him the upper hand. To make matters worse, when the first guard finished beating him, the second and third followed.

Mason was no match for these men one on one, and he certainly couldn't handle them one after the other. As it stood his lip was busted, his nose spewed blood and his eyes were so swollen, he couldn't see anything but figures.

Covered in his own blood, vomit and spit, he stood up again, wobbling so hard someone could have pushed him and his life would be over.

The man was about to finish him, when the guard who pulled Mason out of the cell got a call on his radio, requesting the whereabouts of Mason Louisville. This confused him because everyone knew about the match and knew what Dragon ordered.

So what changed?

After all, Dragon paid a lot of money to see Mason punished and killed. So who had more power than Dragon?

"That's enough," The Guard said. "They want him upstairs."

Upon those words, Mason passed out.

When Mason opened his swollen eyes again, he was in the backseat of a car. He could barely see, with the exception of a little light shining through his lids. But he did know that Whoyawanmetabe was in the car, because he recognized his accent.

Still exhausted and very relieved, he passed out again.

242   *By T. Styles*

WAR 3: THE LAND OF THE LOU'S

243

CHAPTER TWENTY-SIX

Jersey had a heavy chain around her neck and a vacuum cleaner in hand while Dragon sat on the bed naked, with his dick in hand. As she pushed the cleaner around, he directed her where to go and stroked himself every so often. "Vacuum over near the drawer," he instructed, just to watch her cheeks jiggle.

She did as he pleased, the chain jingling behind her.

"Vacuum over by the closet," he demanded next.

Again, she did as he pleased.

This act had nothing to do with cleanliness. Dragon derived a sick level of pleasure by watching not only someone he had been obsessed with all of his life do whatever he commanded, but also a beautiful black woman.

"Put the vacuum up and dust the floorboards."

She placed the cleaner in the closet in the kitchen, grabbed a rag off of the dresser and dropped to her hands and knees. When she did, her flower opened up causing him to become so

By *T. Styles*

stiff it was painful. He could see her entire pussy from the back.

"Crawl over here," he dictated, not being able to take much more.

She complied and quickly sucked his dick nice and slow the way he liked. Her eyes remained on him and she pretended to derive much pleasure from the act, although she hated him more than he could imagine.

"Get on the bed, nigger," he said, which always sent chills up her spine.

Still, she lay face up, with her legs open and waited for him to penetrate her womb. The moment the tip was inside of her pussy, she went into actress mode. As he tugged on the chain she said, "You feel so fucking good, master," she moaned licking her lips. "Real good."

"You like this dick, bitch?" He said, pumping in and out of her roughly. "You like it better than any nigger dick you've had in your life?"

"Yes," she nodded. "I love it so much more, master...and I'm about to cum. I'm about...um...your dirty whore is about to cum now!"

Hearing those words, within two seconds, Dragon whipped his dick out and exploded his thick cream onto her belly. And when he was done, as if a director said cut, she jumped out of bed, stomped toward the bathroom and slammed the door.

"What's wrong with you?!" He yelled, wiping his dick with a towel on the dresser. "Jersey, what's wrong with you?"

Dragon was sitting up in bed, watching television with Jersey who sat next to him. She was so stiff, that her body mechanics resembled that of a mannequin. When he gazed over and saw her face, he grabbed the remote and put the show on pause.

Taking a deep breath he said, "Are you gonna be like this forever?"

Silence.

He crossed his arms over his chest. "I know this isn't your idea of a family, but you don't know how much I've been wanting this."

She looked over at him. "And what exactly is *this*?"

By T. Styles

He frowned. "You and me to be together forever."

"But, Dragon, I—"

"Don't bring up your sons again." He sat up on the side of the bed, his back toward her, his gaze on the window. "I don't want to hear about them grown ass men anymore."

"I know you remember how things were when we were in foster care. But we adults now. I have responsibilities. I have people who care about me and—"

"And if you care about them, like you say you do, then you need to stay here with me *willingly*. As you can see with Mason, and even the rape charges I had dropped on your sons, that I'm able to do many things. I'm able to shake things up in your life, in a way you could never imagine. Is that what you want?"

He got up and walked toward the door. "I'm about to grab a beer." He opened it. "You want something?"

She shook her head.

When he was gone, she used the time to think clearly. Her sons were on the way, that she was certain, based on what Mason said earlier. And as always nothing meant more to her than protecting them. It was the reason she reached out to Dragon in the first place, when she felt Banks was about to kill them all. And it was the reason she would have to save them again.

After taking a quick moment to pluck some ideas out of the ether, she walked to her drawer and grabbed a few things. Then she moved into the bathroom just as Dragon was coming back inside the room. When he saw her gone he yelled, "Don't be in there too long. We gotta start season two."

Silence.

He looked at the closed door and placed two beers on the end table. "And I bought you something to drink anyway. I figured it'll help you lighten the fuck up."

Silence.

He sat on the bed, with his back against the headboard and looked at the door. "Are you okay in there?"

Silence.

He frowned. "Jersey, are you okay?"

Silence.

He was about to get up and kick the bathroom door in when she walked out. "I'm fine." She smiled. "Just had to use it right quick."

248   *By T. Styles*

He observed her closely, trying to detect lies. "I thought you fell into the toilet for a minute."

She chuckled once for his efforts at humor but that was all she could provide. "Nope...just needed to use it that's all." She sat on the bed, with her back against the headboard. "You gonna give it to me?"

He frowned. "Give you what?"

She pointed at the beer bottle. "The drink."

"Oh...uh...yeah." He reached over on the table, grabbed it and handed it to her. "I'm over here tripping. Forgot I brought you something."

"It's all good." She took a huge gulp. "Turn the show back on."

He nodded, observed her for a second more and complied. Something felt off but the last thing he wanted was to rock the boat if she was finally coming around to seeing things his way.

The show was five minutes in when she said, "You know I never came right?"

He looked at her, his head tilted a little to the right. "Came where?"

"When we had sex." She placed the bottle on the table near her. "Not even just now." She sighed. "I always wondered why. I mean, I've been satisfied before with my husband and even my ex-boyfriend...but with you, never have I been satisfied sexually."

He turned the TV off. "How you sound?" He smiled. "I had you calling my name when we went to the beach that day. When we used to—"

"We were filming remember? We were on set. That's the thing you never got about me...although I cared about you, most of what you deemed as love was just me trying to keep mommy and daddy happy. It was just me trying to make a good movie. But I'm being real now, you never satisfied me, Dragon. Not once."

He glared. "I know what you doing." He pointed at her.

She frowned. "What you talking about?"

"You want me to crash your jaw in. You want me to get angry so you'll have enough energy to try to escape." He laughed and raked his hair back with his fingers. "The funny part is, even if I did allow you to take me there, you will never leave me again." He took a large sip. "Until I'm done with you."

"I know that as fact." She shrugged. "So why would I do that?" She threw her hands up. "You have me right where you want. My kids aren't allowed to come over. My husband is locked up. If

By *T. Styles*

I come at you about anything, you'll have the boys arrested again and kill Mason in jail. So tell me why would I anger the man who has proven he has control of my life? Why can't it be, that if you want me here, that I simply must start telling you my truth?"

He observed her closely and took another sip.

Part of him wanted to beat her blindly, like he had before. But then he would be forced into feeling guilty for days like he did every other time he'd gone too far. She was precious to him. She was also the one woman he tried to hold back his anger for, to keep her in his life.

So he took a deep breath, put the beer down and got up.

"Where you going?" She asked.

"I'll be back." He walked into the bathroom.

With the door closed, he sat on the edge of the tub in complete rage. Slamming his hands over his mouth, he screamed into his palms. His skin reddened as he released pinned up frustration. He never wanted or loved a woman more than Jersey and yet she always appeared out of reach.

Standing up, he opened the medicine cabinet, grabbed his gun from the hidden compartment and placed it against his neck before pulling the trigger.

BOOM!

Blood and flesh splattered on the shower's wall.

The moment he felt the bullet penetrate his neck, his eyes flew open.

This was not supposed to happen!

The gun was always empty!

Scared and confused, his body fell forward into the tub and Jersey walked into the bathroom door, calmly.

"I'm sorry," she said softly, sitting on the toilet.

His eyes were wide and it was the first time she saw him afraid. "Why?" He mouthed, as blood continued to pour out the wound and down the drain.

"At my thirteenth birthday party, you bought me a pretty black doll," she smiled awkwardly for the moment. "And I remember looking at it and thinking, it's so pretty, I don't want it. But it wasn't because I was too old to play with dolls, which I was by the way," she recalled. "It was because it was too perfect. Too innocent. And I didn't want anything perfect or innocent in a

By T. Styles

house so depraved." She scooted up a little on the seat. "But you took my rejection personally and you ran away from the table and into daddy's' room."

"Please help me," he mouthed.

"And I followed you," she continued, caring less about his pleas. "I followed you because whenever you didn't get your way, you would always run off. And I had to figure out where you went. Mainly because whenever you would disappear, you would return later with a look of peace on your face. And I wanted that type of peace for myself." She took a deep breath.

"So imagine my surprise when I saw you grab daddy's gun from under the bed, place it to your temple and pull the trigger." She laughed softly and then quieted immediately. "I didn't know if you carried that bad habit into your adult life or not, until I recalled the arguments we had since I'd been here, and how you would go into this bathroom, and come out, all-better again. So I placed bullets in the gun today, and waited to make you angry."

His eyes were rolling back into his head.

"I didn't own a weapon, but my husband does, so I grabbed his. At first I was going to blast your brains out when you were asleep. But why should I do the dirty work when you could do it yourself. It was a gamble that the bullets would fit, but it was a gamble I was willing to take."

His blood continued to pour down the drain.

"I really am sorry, Dragon. I loved you. But I love my family more. And for that you must die."

By T. Styles

CHAPTER TWENTY-SEVEN

Minnie woke up after a huge bump jolted her from sleep.

When she sat up, moaning a little in the process, she was surprised to see Arlyndo driving her in a truck she didn't recognize. One minute they were in a nice hotel in Virginia, which had become their home for months, and the next she couldn't recall leaving.

Had he drugged her?

Sitting up as best she could without hurting her leg she focused on him. A fresh cast had replaced her old one, although she told the doctor she believed she could walk.

There was a growing dissention between Arlyndo and the doctor. He had realized that Mason was looking for his son, and so the Doc threatened to let Mason know where Arlyndo was, if he ever contacted him again.

And that's when Arlyndo made his next move.

To flee.

"Bae, what's going on?"

He looked back at her and smiled. "How you feel?"

"I'm fine I guess." She sat in the middle of the seat and scooted up a little. "But...where you taking us?" She looked around. Although she didn't recognize anything in particular, she could tell that they were far from home.

"I thought about things, with your father and mine, and I finally realized what I have to do."

"Okay...so are you gonna tell me?" She gave him half a smile.

"I don't want you upset."

Her heart beat heavily. "I'm not gonna lie...you scaring me."

"I don't mean to."

"Then give it to me straight."

"We going to Mexico."

Her jaw dropped but she quickly pulled up her lip. She knew her man enough to know that if he had the slightest idea that she didn't want to be with him, or trust his leadership, that he would make things worse.

"So is your plan for us to stay a little while? Like...until things blow over?"

"No."

"Then what is the plan, Arlyndo? Because we can't be in Mexico forever. We have family and—"

"The only thing or person I care about in the world is you. That's it. I could give a fuck less about anybody else."

"Baby...please listen to me...I don't wanna...I mean...I don't wanna go without seeing my mother and father. I ain't got no problem being with you, I swear I don't...but if you take me away forever, it's going to tear my family apart. I haven't even told them that I'm okay. If you love me you would understand this."

"Nah."

"Nah? But...I mean...aren't you listening to me?"

He pulled over to the side of the road, got out and crawled in the backseat, slamming the door shut. He looked like a madman. "Think about it for a second...if Banks was willing to move you out the country, what would make him change his mind if he finds out my father really did try to kill you?"

"I won't tell him."

"IT DOESN'T FUCKING MATTER!" Arlyndo roared. "Now...now...I'm sorry I had to yell but..." he touched her leg and she jumped. Taking a deep breath he said, "The last person I want you to be afraid of is me. But if that's what it takes to keep you, I guess I'll do just that."

She touched his hand. "Arlyndo, please don't—"

He yanked away from her and took his position in the driver's seat again. With a scowl on his face, he continued to drive down the road. Minnie knew she had to make a move but she didn't know how. When they came to a slow crawl, she had an idea.

She loved, Arlyndo, she truly did, but her best friend Nasty Natty was right. He was a special kind of crazy that she wasn't equipped to deal with just yet. Suddenly she felt stupid for running to him instead of away from him but it was too late. She needed to take a chance for her life. So when the time was right, she pushed the truck door open and rolled out into the middle of the street.

A speeding Porsche, occupied by a white man on his phone, stopped inches before rolling over her body. Falling would have been the least of Minnie's problems but there was another. After pushing the truck door open, she fell the wrong way, causing her head to slam against the ground, rendering her unconscious.

Arlyndo, in fear of it all, quickly pulled over and jumped out.

A few cars stopped in Minnie's path to prevent her from being crushed and there was a growing crowd approaching with camera phones in hand.

"Is she okay?" Porsche driver asked.

"She's fine!" Arlyndo dropped to his knees and held Minnie. The gash on her scalp looked serious. "Bae, are you okay?"

She was unconscious as blood poured from her head.

"Maybe we should call 911," A woman in a soccer mom van suggested.

"She'll be fine," he glared, looking around at the crowd that continued to grow. "Just leave us alone!"

"I'm calling the police," Soccer mom replied, dialing the number.

The way things were going, in a little while the police were sure to be on the scene. It wouldn't take them long to realize he had kidnapped her against her will. So while holding Minnie in his lap, he whipped out his cell phone and called the people he could always count on.

His family.

CHAPTER TWENTY-EIGHT

Banks leaned against his car, until the front door of the townhome he was parked in front of opened. Within seconds, with hunched over shoulders, Spacey walked out and down the steps slowly.

Standing in front of Banks, he tucked his hands into his pockets and sighed. He looked like a child preparing to get scolded instead of a grown man. "Pops..." he squinted. "What you...what you doing out here?"

"I came for you," he smiled.

Spacey nodded. "You lost a lot of weight." He looked at his face. "Been going through a lot?"

Banks looked down at himself and thought about the question. It was hard to answer. "Been through more than I would wish on my worst enemies. And that's a fact."

"Why?"

He sighed deeply. "You know, when we came back to Baltimore, I knew you weren't going to stay. I knew the island was too much for you and I was okay with your decision to leave."

"How did you know I would be here though?"
He shrugged. "I didn't even know you had this address."

Banks laughed. "You are important to me." He touched his shoulder. "And when it comes to you kids, I go ape. I must know everything. I guess that's my problem."

"If you knew I wasn't going back to the island, why did you let me come?"

"Because I was wrong, Spacey. There are things I wanted to do in my life, when it came to you boys but...but I have to remember that you are men who have a right to make your own decisions. And that I can't force what I want on you. As long as you are safe...that's the only time I go insane."

"You scaring me."

Banks stood straight up and held Spacey tightly. With a hand behind his head, he whispered in his ear. "Harris is dead. And Minnie dead too."

Banks felt Spacey's body weaken into his arms, which is why he used the firm hold. He knew he would fall to pieces and didn't want him hitting the ground. Instead he held him tighter, refusing to let him go. Within seconds Spacey released a wail so loud, that the big pretty girl that Spacey was staying with in the townhouse, rushed outside.

She was a chocolate beauty with deep-set eyes and a curvaceous frame. "Is everything alright?" She yelled concerned at what she was seeing. Banks was certain that Spacey had no doubt given her an earful about their lives.

But he didn't care.

"I have him," Banks assured her. "Go back in the house."

She looked at them a few seconds longer and then obeyed.

For five more minutes, no other sound passed between them, other than Spacey's cries. His reaction forced Banks to relive the pain all over again, but he held it together because it wasn't about him.

It was about his oldest.

Besides, the agony he felt over losing two children would never leave his soul. And so he would have to become highly accustomed to its darkness, as if it were a friend.

When Spacey was done, he looked at Banks and wiped his eyes. Banks told him how they died, using the little information he knew.

262

"You want me to go back with you?" He took a deep breath. His face bloodshot red. "To...to help you tell ma?"

"No, son." Banks looked over his shoulder at the townhouse. "I want you to stay here, with your friend."

Spacey nodded, although he wasn't expecting that answer. He was certain that Banks would use his authority like he had in the past and force him on the aircraft. But Banks was growing and trying desperately to be a different man.

"You love her?" Banks nodded toward the house.

He shrugged. "I don't know...I mean...I haven't thought that far out."

"You're young, that part is true. But don't spend a lifetime with somebody you don't care about. It makes for a hard existence."

Spacey nodded, hating the fact that he may have been referring to his mother.

Banks hugged him again. "I have to go. I'm leaving tomorrow but I had to stop here first." He looked at the house and back at him. "You take care of yourself, Spacey. I'm proud of you for standing your ground with me. It was something I waited too late to do with my father."

Banks hugged him once more, climbed in his car and drove away.

By T. Styles

CHAPTER TWENTY-NINE

Megan Jones walked into the front door of her partner's house. She hadn't heard from him all day, which was his right but it didn't stop her from worrying. There was one problem. Megan and Dragon had carried on an extensive love affair for years until some months back, when he expressed to her that it was over. This was about the same time that he found Jersey and wanted her back in his life.

Despite their bond being over, Megan never got over him and she never got over hope that they would one day be reunited. And as a result, they talked to each other most mornings and he always replied back.

So where was he now?

Why hadn't she heard from him?

After walking through the living room, she moved back toward the bedroom, some place she'd been many times before. When she smelled a familiar odor, that she learned how to discern as an officer, she drew her weapon.

Her heart rocked when she realized something was deathly wrong. Her only thought at the moment was if the crime was intentional or accidental. People died due to mishaps all the time.

Could the same thing have happened to her partner? Otherwise known as the love of her life?

When she walked through the bedroom and found nothing, she came upon the closed bathroom door. Slowly she turned the knob and opened it before walking inside. Confused, it took all of a few seconds to see Dragon's graying body, lying in the bathtub with a gun in hand.

She dropped the weapon she was carrying and climbed into the tub with the corpse, weeping loudly. She was so taken aback, that she didn't see the figure walking up behind her from the moment she crossed the threshold.

Jersey hadn't left the house, because she knew her family was coming and wanted them to be able to find her.

Megan quickly looked up and saw Jersey. "Who...who are you?"

"What are you doing here?" Jersey asked.

"Who the fuck are you?!" Megan screamed hating herself for dropping her weapon.

"Does it matter?" Jersey shrugged. "Let's talk about what you should be thinking about in this

266   *By T. Styles*

moment. And that is, what can you say, to convince me to let you go?"

"You're Jersey. Aren't you?"

Silence.

"Listen, all I want to do is take his body and give him the proper burial he deserves," Megan continued.

"He doesn't deserve anything. So that should make your work easier."

Megan took a deep breath. "Look, he...he told me about you. Even when I didn't want to hear about you, he told me how much he loved you. So I know if this happened it wasn't your fault."

"You don't know nothing 'bout me! You don't know how this man terrorized and scared me, when all I wanted was to be with my family. You don't know how he made me have sex with him, even when my body was in pain from the last time he violated me." She sniffled. "So say whatever you want, but I know he didn't share those things with you!"

"You're right. I didn't hear about those things. But let's be honest. What are you going to do? You can't kill a police officer and expect to stay out of prison. But I can help you. If...if you let me go, I promise I will—"

BOOM!

Jersey shot her in the face using Mason's gun. Afterwards she dropped to her knees and cried. She was officially a full-blown-murderer. One from secondhand fire, by stuffing Dragon's gun with bullets and the second by her own hand.

"Ma, what happened?" Derrick asked walking into the bathroom with a cane, seeing the bloody scene. "What you do?"

Jersey turned around and looked up at him from the floor. Behind him were also Patterson and Howard. And within seconds, Mason appeared in the doorway, with a face so destroyed, she almost didn't recognize him.

Still, it didn't stop Jersey from jumping in his arms.

It had been a long day disposing of Dragon and Megan's bodies, and Mason realized that burying corpses was only the start of their troubles. Someone would come looking for the officers and he was certain that the clean up job they did would not be enough to throw off detectives on a mission to find their own.

Standing in front of his family, who were all seated on the living room sofa in their house, Mason took a deep breath. "We have to leave."

"Where can we go that they won't find us?" Jersey asked.

"That island." Mason said seriously. "We need to get there and we need to get there before they smell two dead cops." He paused and dragged a hand down his battered face. "You know, I always thought Banks' island was the land of the Lou's but now I realize it's here, in Baltimore, and now we can't stay."

"But how we gonna get there?" Jersey asked, finally agreeing that it was time to flee.

Mason took a deep breath. "We have to tell you a few things but leave that part to me."

Jersey was washing dishes when Mason came into the kitchen, a look of seriousness on his face. It pained her to see the bruises he succumbed to in jail, knowing that it was part her fault. On the other hand, he had once beaten her just as badly and she looked the same, so it could also be considered justified.

He leaned up against the doorway, arms folded over his chest.

She took a deep breath and turned around. Wiping her hands with the towel she said, "We were in foster care together."

"You told me that already. I need more."

"We...we were forced to, to have sex with each other. All of the kids were actually and..." she shrugged. "It was a rough life, Mason. That I never fully got over. I mean, Dragon was a monster but he was made that way. We all were."

He stepped into the kitchen...closer. "Why didn't you tell me?"

"You didn't ask." She shrugged. "You never cared about my past. And I think you played into the master and servant thing like he did."

"I'm nothing like him."

"You're worse!" She cried. "You're my husband and all you wanted was me to have children and, and, you didn't stop to think that maybe I was a real person." She placed her hands over her heart. "That maybe I had emotions. You treated

270 *By* T. *Styles*

me exactly like he did. Except you made me your wife. And now I'm a monster."

"You not a monster."

She smiled. "Don't you get it yet? You don't know anything about me. I enjoyed taking his life, Mason. And if I had to take another, I'd gladly do it again."

CHAPTER THIRTY

Banks and Rev sat at a bar enjoying two cold beers. Banks had recently gotten his beard shaped up and looked more like himself. Now, it was just his eyes that were dark and full of pain.

The establishment wasn't that crowded, which was perfect for an important conversation. "You know she's not gonna let this go right?" Rev said looking over at him. "You should have killed her."

"I know," Banks nodded. "Just didn't want any..." he took a deep breath. "...I didn't want any more blood on my hands. Too many niggas died and...I just gotta...I need peace right now to keep my mind straight. I feel like karma sat on me and because of it I lost my...I..." He took a huge gulp of beer and the glass came down heavy on the bar.

"I don't know what you going through, but everybody in the game, everybody who signed a verbal contract of sorts, has basically put their life on the line in the name of the streets. And your kids weren't a part of that. So don't blame yourself for their deaths."

Banks still felt heavy. "I hear you."

By T. Styles

Rev nodded. "And Nidia, you see, if ever there was somebody who should have died on contact it should've been her. She will never let you tie her up, reject her and then get away. That woman thrives on war. You said so yourself. You even told me your father engrained that in your mind repeatedly when he ran the streets."

Banks nodded. "He did. And I thought about killing her and getting it over with, but my son's staying in Baltimore. My wife's people live in the town. So I gotta make smarter moves for them."

Rev didn't agree but he had to respect the boss. "Just so you know, I caught up with Johnson finally. Took care of him after I found out he killed our men guarding the plane. Turned out he was working for Mason."

Banks smiled and shook his head. "Can't trust nobody." He paused. "What about Cliff?"

"Gave him the money like you said to get out of town," he paused. "I don't think he knew Mason didn't die in that rec center after the bomb. He seemed spooked out when he found out he was alive. Guess he was afraid that Mason would kill him for betraying him and working for you." He sighed. "So what now?"

He took a deep breath. "Me and Shay going to the island and then I'm gonna tell Bet."

"Tell Bet what?"

"About the kids."

Rev sat the beer on the bar and positioned his stool so he could look at him. "She doesn't know that her kids...I mean..."

"I didn't want Joey going through her pain alone."

"But it's been months."

"Don't make this harder than it already is, man. I know it was fucked up on my part. But I know my wife, my son wouldn't be able to handle her alone if she knew about the kids."

"I'm sorry, boss. But...damn..."

"I know." Banks took a deep breath. "But anyway, I'm here to apologize to you for when you tried to...I mean...when you wanted to help me. And let me know Mason was alive. Although that shit still fucking up my head about your father."

"No apologies necessary."

Banks nodded. "I wish you told me about my mother and your father earlier. I wish you came clean." He pointed at him. "But your loyalty was enough to make amends."

Rev nodded.

By T. Styles

"What ever happened to your father anyway?" Banks continued.

"He died of AIDS in prison...about a year after he killed your mother. Met some woman who was using and then...I guess she was sick and he was sick and one thing led to another." He shrugged. "The information they gave me was in pieces so I had to draw my own conclusions on the rest."

"I always wondered what I would do if I ever saw the man who murdered my mother. Looked for him and everything. Guess shit ain't always packaged neatly. But on my kids, had I saw the man you call father, I would've blasted his brains out in front of his own mother. I swear to God."

"I respect that," Rev nodded, taking a sip.

Silence sat between them a bit longer.

"So...what news you got for me on Mason?" Banks asked.

"Went by the house they stayed at and they gone. Looks like they left in a hurry too. Front door wide open."

"What the fuck?"

"I heard they may be wanted for questioning about some cops. Not sure if it's true or not." He shrugged. "Right now it's just street talk you know?"

Banks nodded.

"So what time you leaving for the island?" Rev asked.

"In an hour. I released the men who were guarding the plane and Shay is already there, waiting on me. I'm just tying up a few things before we head out." He paused. "I gotta be honest though, I'm not looking forward to dealing with Bet. She been unstable...like my mother when I was a kid but I ain't got no choice you know? She's my wife."

"You sound like you thinking about divorce."

"Even if I made a decision to do something like that, she'd always be taken care of. But I don't know if she's the one. At the same time she gave me kids and made my dream come true."

Rev nodded.

"Anyway," Banks drank what was left in his glass. "I need you to look after things here for me."

"This means I got my job back?" Rev joked.

"You never lost it." Banks shook his hand. "Thanks for everything, friend. I'll be in touch."

Rev smiled. "Give Bet my best."

"I'll do that."

By T. Styles

Bet sat at the kitchen table eating gumbo from the day before. She was buttering a piece of cornbread that she made moments earlier when Oswalda walked into the kitchen.

Standing next to her she said, "You seem like you been getting way better lately." She stroked her hair. "That's good Mrs. Wales. That's real good."

Bet smiled.

Although the expression was that of kindness, something in Bet's spirit had grown weary of Oswalda. For starters, ever since Banks left months ago, Oswalda seemed to make her, her primary focus. Her only focus. As a result, Bet couldn't get any rest from her. She was always standing in corners, watching, observing. As if she was wanting or begging her to act out again.

"I want you to know, that it's okay to be who you are."

"What does that mean?" Bet placed a piece of bread into her mouth.

Oswalda shrugged. "You don't have to be perfect with me. Of course I know Joey wants you to be the best version of yourself. Since you are his mother and all. But that's just 'cause he's scared. But for me you're free to say and do as you feel."

Bet chewed her bread quietly.

"I want to hear the voices out loud again." Oswalda continued to stroke Bet's hair. "I want to hear what the voices are telling you, that you don't want anybody else to know about." She walked behind Bet and began massaging her shoulders. "Let them come out, Mrs. Wales. Let them be free."

Bet's heart rate climbed and her forehead felt clammy. She had worked so hard to maintain her grace and it was fucking her up that somebody was trying to seduce her cuckoo out the clock.

"Oswalda, I'm fine." She got up and walked toward the sink. For a second she stood in front of it, in an attempt to shake off the Nunez daughter's energy, but nothing seemed to work.

Oswalda was right on her heels. Belly to back. "I have you, Mrs. Wales. Like always I have you."

"But I don't need you to protect me."

Oswalda hugged her from behind. "But I want to." She kissed the back of her neck. "It's all I've ever wanted to do since the first day we met. Can't you see how much I'll make a good daughter-in-law?"

Bet turned around. "Please leave me be!"

Oswalda grabbed her shoulders. "But I can't! Because you—" Suddenly Oswalda's eyes flew open.

Stunned, she released the hold on Bet and took two steps back. When Oswalda looked down at her stomach, she saw a gaping hole in her flesh. Placing her hand on the wound, it was soon obvious that her hand was covered in blood.

Bet dropped the knife she used to butter her cornbread moments earlier and covered her mouth with her fingertips. "I'm...I'm so sorry."

Oswalda hit the floor. "Why?"

"Ma, you still wanna go to the beach before we—" Joey paused after walking into the kitchen, only to see Oswalda on the floor, covering her stomach. His eyes flew open. "Ma, what happened?!"

"She...she wouldn't stop...I just wanted peace of mind and she...she wouldn't stop."

"Oswalda, mom wants you to—" Tobias paused in the doorway when he saw his sister's condition. Rushing up to her and dropping to his knees, he looked at the Wales family. "Why did you do this?" He asked hysterically. "What happened?"

Joey ran over to Bet and rushed her out of the doorway.

"YOU KILLED THE WRONG MAN'S DAUGHTER!" Tobias yelled. "DO YOU HEAR ME? YOU KILLED THE WRONG MAN'S DAUGHTER!"

Five minutes later Joey and Bet were inside a steel door bedroom. It was a room Banks had planned to use to build his explosives and so it was reinforced. Although they were securely inside at the moment, it was obvious that their peace would be short-lived, evident by the banging on the door from the Nunez family.

While Bet sat on the sofa, Joey tried desperately to reach Banks to tell him what was happening. But each call fell into voicemail, which frustrated him beyond belief.

After the eighth attempt to contact Banks, Joey walked over to the couch in the room and sat next to his mother. Every so often the door would rock, as obscenities were yelled at them

280   *By* *T. Styles*

from the Nunez family members who were trying to get inside.

Both knew their lives would be over immediately if that door came tumbling down.

"Open the door!" Rosa wept. "I just want to...I just want to talk to you."

"Then why Tobias grab a gun then?" Joey yelled. "Tell me that?"

Tobias laughed softly. It was a guttural laugh that sounded sinister and dark. "Open the door...if it was all an accident like you claim, why run and hide? Come out and talk to us. It's all we want."

"We're not opening that door!" Bet yelled. "Go away! Leave us alone! Banks will be back to—"

"Wake up you stupid, bitch," Tobias said softly. "No one is coming back for you. And unless you want to die of starvation, I suggest you let us in now!"

"Leave us alone!" Bet begged.

"He's coming to reclaim what's his," Rosa said. "You will be sorry you killed his daughter. You will all be sorry."

CHAPTER THIRTY-ONE

Banks had fired up all cylinders on the plane and was about to take off in a matter of minutes. Shay, nervous to fly, walked up behind him and sat in the co-pilot chair. Her body trembled and it wasn't until that moment that he had any inclination that she was fearful.

He looked over at her. "You okay?"

She shook her head slowly from left to right. "I ain't never been in a plane before." She took a deep breath. "When Harris explained to me that we would be going to Wales Island, when mama and dad were alive, I would fall into full blown panic attacks just thinking about it."

He placed his hand on her thigh. "Nothing will happen to you. Not while I'm the pilot. I've done this many times."

She nodded, swallowed the lump in her throat and looked out the window in front of them. "Dad, will, will something happen to me since I...since I killed somebody? Like, will...will I go to hell or something?"

He took a deep breath. Not only because of the question but also because of her using the word

282   *By T. Styles*

dad. It was too soon to hear the epithet in his opinion but he had to understand how important it was to her.

He also knew when she committed murder to save him that it would come back and haunt her somehow. But he hoped he would have some time to get her over it. To show her that despite such a heinous crime, he would sincerely take her into his family, because she showed loyalty when it counted most.

But he wanted to do it later. Besides, they hadn't gotten off ground and although he knew how to fly better than most knew how to walk, heavy emotions before launching an aircraft was a hindrance.

"You did what you did for me. And you did what you did for our family. Back in the day people committed murder all the time as a means to survive. Now that doesn't mean you should kill on sight in the future. But when it comes down to you or them, you better make the smartest decision." He smiled. "Let it go, Shay."

She nodded. "But what about God?"

He shrugged. "I can't talk much on that. But from what I'm told *He* knows your heart." He took a deep breath. "Now are you ready to go?"

She nodded. "Yes...uh...I think so."

"Do me a favor, go downstairs and grab a few bottles of water. I forgot to put some in the cooler up here." He turned the heat on. "I'm going to—" He paused when he saw Spacey's car rushing up to the strip. "I'll be back, Shay." Banks exited the plane and met his son. "What are you doing here?"

Spacey activated the alarm on his Benz and took a deep breath. "I tried to call you before I came."

"My battery's dead...now why you here?"

"I'm coming with you."

Banks shook his head. "No...no...no, son. I want you to let me handle this matter with your mother alone. I don't want this on your heart and—"

"We family," Spacey said passionately. "And I'm a Wales." He stepped closer. "Plus...I mean...yesterday was the first time you respected me as a man. I mean, *really* respected me. It was the first time you talked to me like I'm...like I'm not a kid and so I'm continuing the tradition by making grown man decisions right now."

Banks smiled. "Don't be misled, Spacey. I'm far from a changed man. But I'm trying."

284 *By T. Styles*

"And that's all I ever wanted," Spacey shrugged. "I'm coming with you. Besides, how you gonna take to the skies without your co-pilot?"

Banks pulled him into a manly hug and five minutes later they were on the plane. But the moment they walked into the aircraft, both of them paused when they saw Shay holding two bottles of water with Mason Louisville standing behind her with a gun to her back.

His feet were bleeding profusely.

Banks stumbled backwards.

The rumor was right.

"The plan was to stay downstairs...but she came down and saw me." Mason paused. "Normally I could've hidden myself below the plane but I got a whole crew this time."

What was he talking about?

Prior to that moment it was speculative if Mason were alive or not. But now he was seeing his long lost friend with his own eyes. There was a cocktail of emotions that Banks felt and it was all so hard to describe.

"What you doing here, Louisville?" Banks asked.

"I come back from the dead and that's all you gotta say to me?" Mason smiled. "I mean, considering our past I deserve a little better don't you think?"

"You tried to kill me and hurt my family, and you want me to give a fuck about you?"

"They alive ain't they?"

"Nah...they not!"

Mason looked back and yelled, "Howard and Arlyndo...bring her up!"

Banks was confused but within ten seconds, the Louisville duo came from below, holding Minnie. It took everything in Banks' body to remain on his feet upon seeing his daughter.

Banks stood on his knees as he held Minnie's hand tightly into his own. She was lying on one of the beds in the aircraft and he had never seen a more beautiful sight in all his life. Her head was busted and patched with gauze, and one of her legs was awkwardly smaller than the other.

By T. Styles

Courtesy of the cast, which although now removed, had been on the limb for far too long.

But she was alive.

His baby girl was alive!

There was something else. Her eyes also told him that she matured and he could only guess why. She had seen a lot of things. Seen a lot of blood shed and saw two families that claimed to love each other, do their best to tear each other apart.

Standing behind him as he spoke to his daughter were Spacey, Shay, Mason, Jersey, Patterson, Howard, Derrick and Arlyndo.

"Daddy, I did something that I want to tell you about," she said as a tear fell backwards. "Something that I'm ashamed to—"

"The letter came back," he smiled. "Return to sender."

She tilted her head. "What...how?"

"No postage. You didn't put a stamp on it."

She looked at him for a few seconds longer and giggled quietly in relief. The audience didn't know the details, so all they could do was wonder what the inside joke was all about.

He kissed the top of her hand. "I can't believe you're alive," Banks smiled brighter. "I...I can't believe, after everything, you're actually here."

"I missed you so much, daddy. I missed mama too." She reached out for him with both arms and he hugged her tightly. She looked over at her brother Spacey and smiled. He winked at her and smiled back. "How's everybody? How's Joey? Mama? And Harris?"

He separated from her.

The audience shuffled a little, all knowing something she didn't. That Harris Kirk Wales was dead. Arlyndo was the only one in the pack that didn't have full information.

Banks decided against talking about Harris just yet. "How did you...I mean...where were you all this time?"

She smiled. "Arlyndo...he...he came back and found me in the ditch."

Banks looked back at Arlyndo and then Minnie. He still didn't like him, nor would he ever, but he thanked God for his obsession with finding his flesh and blood. "But there was another girl...who...who was wearing the same clothes you had on," Banks continued. "I thought you were dead because of it."

288   *By T. Styles*

Minnie frowned. "I don't understand."

Everyone looked at Arlyndo, knowing he alone held the answer.

"She was...somebody I ain't fuck with like that," Arlyndo responded, tucking his hands into his back pockets.

"So you killed someone else, just to throw me off?!" Banks slowly stood up and approached him.

Mason was stunned. He didn't know his son was capable of murder.

"Do you know what I been through since I thought my daughter was dead?" Banks continued. "Do you have any idea, Arlyndo?!"

"Easy, man," Mason said with a hand firmly to the center of Banks' chest. "That's my son."

Banks slapped Mason's hand away. "Yeah, well this nigga sent me through a storm with making me think my daughter was dead." He pointed at Arlyndo with a stiff finger.

Arlyndo took one step closer to Banks. "I thought you would take her from me and—"

"And what?" Banks yelled. "You kill somebody else to throw me off? She's not your fucking property!" He pointed at her. "And if you think you can control her by bossing her around, or trying to rule her life, you gonna lose her!" He pointed at him.

"You mean like you do Mrs. Bet?" Arlyndo continued.

Everyone present gasped.

He was speaking big facts.

"He's right," Derrick added. "What about you, Banks? Huh? What about all the shit you did? What about cutting my toe off? And me getting shot at your house? You said you loved us and we were like sons to you. But the moment you got into it with Pops, you treated me and my brothers like you ain't know us. And that ain't right! All I wanted to do was make peace." Derrick did all he could to hold back his emotions but it was tough for the young bull.

Banks sighed. "I didn't...I didn't shoot you." He looked downward. "I told you that already." He ran a hand down his face. "And it wasn't me who started that war that night in my dining room. All I wanted was to leave and your father wouldn't allow me."

"I know it wasn't you," Jersey interrupted softly. "Even told my husband. But that doesn't change all that has happened now does it? A lot of people got hurt. A lot of people got killed."

By T. Styles

"Including Linden," Mason glared.

"And Harris," Banks snapped.

"Harris?" Minnie blurted. "What's...what's wrong with Harris?"

"Nothing," Mason lied. "I mean...You know...being locked up."

Everyone shuffled.

"Please stop the fighting," Minnie said softly. "I don't want nobody else hurt in our family. I mean, at one point we all loved each other. Can't we go back to that?"

"We will never be family again," Banks promised looking directly into his ex-best friend's eyes. "Ever."

"I hear no lies here." Mason nodded, arms crossed over his body.

"So what do you want?" Banks asked.

"We being hunted," Mason said. "And I need to get to that island."

Banks laughed. "So you want me to take you to *my* paradise? You sound crazy."

"I been there already, man," Mason said slyly. "Met Oswalda and the whole gang. So if I wanted you dead you would be gone but yet you're still alive."

Banks' heart dropped. "How...what..."

"It doesn't matter," Mason responded. "All I know is this...we have you out numbered. I also heard that you beefing with Nidia. So unless you want her to pull up and blast this fucking plane out the air, I suggest we take flight. Now!"

It was pitch black as Banks piloted the night skies. He could hear Shay weeping in the background due to fright, while Minnie, Jersey and Spacey did their best to console her. Everyone else was relaxing and enjoying the plane ride.

Limping due to his feet being ripped to shreds, Mason flopped into the co-pilot seat in the cockpit. "I can't believe you actually know how to fly this shit. You a nigga from Baltimore and look at you now."

Banks gazed over at him and glared.

"Come on, man," Mason continued. "You can't be mad at me forever."

"Just because you put me in a position where I gotta take you to my haven, don't mean we friends."

Mason raised his foot and rested it on his own knee, while he pulled out glass shards.

"And why you not wearing shoes?"

"Had to leave in a hurry. Dragon's cop friends were coming."

"Who's Dragon? The same nigga who fucked up your face?"

"He ain't a nigga but it's a long story." Mason paused. "And you can lie all you want." He pointed at him. "I know a part of you relieved I'm still alive." He shrugged. "I don't even need a confirmation on that because it's facts."

Banks adjusted the headset he was wearing and sighed. "You should've let me get my family to Wales Island like I wanted. You shouldn't have pushed the issue. I set you up with enough money and coke to last a while. Ain't my fault you a bully with money. You were wrong."

"Maybe." He shrugged. "Maybe not."

"I mean what's your long term plan? You can't possibly believe that I'll allow us to live in harmony on an island I built. You ruined the plans I had for my future, Mason. I can't let that shit slide."

"I don't expect us to regain what we had." He paused. "But the fact of the matter is, I brought you back your daughter, and if you were as tore up as you claimed, I deserve a truce break for now." He picked out another piece of glass from his foot. "Oh, and something is up with that Oswalda girl."

He frowned, still irritated that he had been on his private land and that she didn't tell him. "Why you say that?"

"She acts like one of our kids," he removed another piece of glass. "Like she came from money."

"I don't know about all that."

Mason shrugged. "Maybe you're right." He took out the final piece of glass. "I was always way dumber than you." He wasn't being sarcastic. It was the way he actually felt.

"You know what..." Banks turned to the side, and removed his sneakers and socks. "Jersey, can you bring this nigga that first aid kit over your head?"

She complied and then cleaned and bandaged Mason's bloody feet.

294 *By T. Styles*

When she was done, and rejoined the girls, Banks said, "Here." He handed him his sneakers and socks. "Wear these."

Mason frowned. "But...what about you?"

"I don't need socks and shoes to fly. You need to cover your feet though before they get infected." He paused. "Don't worry...they clean."

Mason slid the socks on and winced. "Wow...the tables turned."

Banks frowned. "What you rapping about now?"

"I remember back in the day when I gave you my shoes and now...look at you."

"You always loved talking about the past. Stay in the present, nigga. It'll treat you much better."

Mason laughed heartily.

Banks laughed too, although he didn't mean to. It was just too good to speak to his old friend, although he'd never let a soul know.

"We got history, nigga," Mason responded. "And after everything we been through, can't nobody take that away."

Banks took a deep breath. "Mason, why did you...why did you tell...why did you tell people my..."

"We went to war, Banks, that's true, but if there's anything I regret it's revealing the secret you entrusted me with. And the moment I let it out, I hated myself for it." He looked straight ahead. "Guess I never got over how shit went down when you..." he looked back at the kids. "...when you broke my heart."

By T. Styles

CHAPTER THIRTY-TWO
JANUARY 1988

B lakeslee was sitting in front of Nikki's door, begging for her to talk to her as she had almost every day, since Angie dragged Nikki out of her house and tossed her in the hallway kicking and screaming.

Blakeslee knew she was inside. She saw her enter earlier but she wouldn't open the door, as she had in the past. Blakeslee had done all she could to get through to Nikki. Nikki didn't even reach out to Blakeslee after her mother was murdered in a liquor store. She thought they were friends, and that surely she would hear from her. But when she didn't, it hurt.

And then there was the awkwardness of what Blakeslee was becoming. She had already begun the transitioning stage by wearing baggy clothing and wearing her hair in two long French braids. She wasn't looking the same.

She was still trying to find out what it meant to be Banks, instead of Blakeslee but it was hard. For starters without Mason, who Blakeslee had been ignoring, she didn't know how to dress or what to wear.

To be honest she never expected her mother, before she died, to allow her to live as a boy. It was the furthest thing from her mind, and yet there she was, living a life that she wasn't prepared to handle.

"You cool?" Mason asked, standing at the stairwell, leaning against the wall. His hands in his coat pockets, a gold chain dripping around his neck. He looked like money.

"Leave me alone," Blakeslee said quietly.

"Come on, man, it's been a minute." He walked over to her. "Like...I mean...how long you staying mad at me?"

She sighed. "What you want?"

"I got some pizza in my crib," he said pointing behind him with his thumb. "You wanna slice? It's a lot and I'm not gonna be able to crush all of it by myself."

Mason had long since given up any long-term goals of making Banks, as she called herself now, his girl again. But it didn't stop him from loving her, and wanting her severely.

At the same time he knew Dennis, who had recently been granted an early release from prison

By T. Styles

mainly due to the press of Angie's murder, couldn't afford to feed her like he wanted. It was hard on a regular person with limited skills to get a job. But a convict would be at the bottom of the list of possible employees.

And so Blakeslee and Dennis were virtually broke.

So Mason tried the one thing he felt would work to reconnect with his friend. Food. "I'm serious, man," Mason begged. "I really can't eat it all. You want some?"

A few minutes later Blakeslee was in Mason's apartment eating hot fresh pizza on the sofa. Since she blamed him for the reason Nikki didn't talk to her anymore, she cut off their relationship immediately. But now as they spent time together again, she forgot how much she enjoyed his company.

As they laughed at an episode of 'The Cosby Show', Mason looked over at her and smiled. She was still so fucking pretty it was hard to digest. He could see where she was trying to change into a boy. And he gave her an E for effort, but it had yet to take hold. Mainly because hormonal therapy was a long ways away for Blakeslee and so she resembled a tomboy more than a full-blown male.

"You want something to drink?" Mason asked.

She grabbed another slice of pizza and nodded. With a mouth full of pepperoni and crust she said, "Yes, please, thank you."

While Blakeslee fell out laughing at Rudy dancing, Mason put a little Strawberry Cisco in the red Kool-Aid and gave it to her. Five minutes later, the TV was off and Blakeslee had lightened up as they continued to enjoy each other's company.

"So, what's going on with your girl?" Mason asked, taking a sip of the same concoction.

She shrugged. "She ain't talking to me. Still mad, you know?"

Mason nodded. "She'll come around."

Her eyes lightened up.

It was the first time someone had talked about Nikki, let alone gave her hope that one-day the pain she felt from not having Nikki in her life would go away. "You...you think so?"

"I know so," Mason promised. "I mean...as long as you know how to please her and stuff like that. But I know you got it."

She gave him her undivided attention. "What...what you mean?"

Mason shrugged. "We gonna be in high school so girls be different 'bout that time in they life. You

300   By T. Styles

gotta know how to make 'em feel and shit. And Nikki, I know for a fact, gonna wanna feel good all the time. 'Cause she real pretty."

"So...so what can I do?"

"Just do it right when ya'll have sex." He shrugged. "'Cause if you don't, she not gonna stay with you, man."

Blakeslee looked around the living room and back at Mason. She was trying desperately to find the recipe to keep Nikki around for life. So she moved closer in the hopes of getting enlightened. "Can you...like help me with that?"

Mason's heart rocked. He was getting closer, he could feel it. "I don't know...I mean...what you talkin' about?"

"Tell me what I gotta do when I get her back."

Mason felt dizzy. He wanted her so badly he was stiffening in a way he never had before. "Just kiss her softly and then, go between her legs and kiss that too. Then you gotta stick it in and stuff like that."

"How you know about that...like what to do?"

Mason shifted a little.

Unfortunately sexual abuse by the hands of his uncle and a few freaky girl babysitters, gave him *way more knowledge than he should have for a boy his age. "I just know. Leave it at that."*

"But I...like I need you to show me, Mason." Blakeslee grabbed his hand. "Please."

Mason swallowed the lump in his throat. "What that mean?"

"Do to me...what I gotta do to her. So she'll like it."

Mason stood up and Blakeslee rose too. "Come with me then."

A few minutes later Blakeslee was lying face up in bed, wearing her light pink bra and panty set. Every limb of her body shivered as she braced herself for whatever was about to happen.

Mason was no better in the moment. And yet this was all his show. He alone was in charge. Slowly he walked over to the bed and sat on the edge. It squeaked. "You don't gotta be scared with me." He paused. "I won't hurt you."

Blakeslee nodded and closed her eyes. "Show me. Show me how to keep her."

Mason took off his jeans and crawled on the bed. Carefully he removed her pink panties and took a deep breath. Then he removed her bra and eyed her palm size breasts as if they were chocolate chip cookies, even licking his lips. He

302   *By T. Styles*

couldn't get over how perfect her body was. More than anything, he wondered why she wanted to be a boy when she was doing such a great job at being a girl.

But he could sense by her closed eyes, that she wanted to separate herself from the act. So his mission was simple. Sex her so good that she would always remember that night, no matter what.

That she would always be in love with him.

Even if she denied it.

"So you gotta...you gotta do this first." He lay on the bed and pushed her legs open wider. Then he pressed the tip of his tongue on her clit and she jumped. "Are you...okay?"

She closed her eyes tighter and nodded. "I'm...I'm fine. You can go 'head."

Slowly he licked her clit and then traced it into her tunnel. Blakeslee did all she could to look at it for what it was, an act, that if possible, would bring her closer to Nikki, but it was hard. And she hadn't expected it to feel so...strange...and so...good...and so dirty, all at the same time.

Mason was so soft and methodic with his tongue flips, that he had her hating herself for responding to a boy when she knew she liked girls.

But in the end her body was unfaithful to what she desired in her heart and so as a result she experienced her first orgasm.

It was so miraculous...

Evident by the way her body trembled and tingled. And how she softly placed a hand on each side of his face and pumped a little when she came. Add to that, a healthy amount of oil had covered her lips.

"Oh...oh my..." she opened her eyes and breathed heavily. "What was...what was that?"

Mason looked up at her, pushed down his boxers and released himself quickly before she changed her mind. He was already rock hard and it was time to finish what he started. Placing his lips beside her ear he said, "And then you have to do this, baby."

He pushed into her slowly and the slickness of her tunnel allowed him a less painful entry.

Upon feeling the pressure of her tunnel widening to accept him fully, Blakeslee's mouth opened and her chin rose to the ceiling. She battled with how to deal with what was happening. How could she look at him again afterwards? How could she look at anyone again, knowing she wanted to be a boy?

304

And then it all made sense.

Somehow, some way, she would make Nikki experience the exact same things, in the exact same way, when the time came. And so, she pretended it was like a class. With Mason as her teacher. So she opened her body by widening her legs and relaxed into Mason's touch.

Mason had no idea that she was trying to learn.

He looked at the widening of her legs as submission, as a hint that she was feeling him after all. His plan was working.

Mason was slow at first, but he wanted her so badly that before long, the young boy in him made himself known and so he humped faster and harder not being able to hold back the urge to bust. Because while he had unfortunately been shown how to do oral on his uncle and a few freaky female babysitters, Blakeslee was his first sexual experience, and he was hers.

Right before he came he moved his mouth toward her ear and said, "I love you." He pumped one more time and said, "Don't leave me. I lovvvveeee...uhhhhhhh." He splashed inside of her body.

Hoping he didn't hurt her, he quickly rolled off of her in embarrassment.

"I'm...I'm sorry," Mason said.

She looked over at him. "It's okay," she whispered.

"I...did I hurt you?" Mason asked.

She shook her head no.

"Can we...can we get back together then?" Mason continued. "I won't...I won't make you...like change your clothes or nothin'."

Blakeslee took a deep breath. "We can never do that again." She leaned over and kissed his cheek. "We can never tell anybody either. I'm sorry."

She grabbed her clothes, got dressed and walked to the doorway. Before stepping out she turned around. "But...I want us to be friends."

Silence.

Mason rolled over with his back faced the door.

Young boy was heated!

Fuck that bitch, is what he was thinking.

But Blakeslee had been transformed and so she no longer wanted to fight. Not only did she know how she wanted Nikki to feel, she also realized she needed him in her life. Forever. "Mason, can we be friends?"

Knowing he couldn't not be cool with her either, he rolled back over and looked at her before taking a deep breath. "Best friends?"

306　　　　　　*By T. Styles*

Blakeslee nodded yes.

"No matter what happens?" Mason continued. "Or like, what girl comes into the picture? Or, um, how much we fight?"

"Best friends no matter what. Nothing will tear us apart. Ever."

CHAPTER THIRTY-THREE

Banks landed safely on Wales Island.

The moment he arrived, and his bare toes nestled into the sand; he was shocked that no one was there to greet him. He figured since his battery died and he failed to charge it, due to the shock with Mason being on the plane, that they were simply unaware he was coming since he couldn't call.

Banks took a deep breath. He knew within seconds he would have to tell his wife the truth about Harris, even though the news was not as bad as he originally felt it was. After all, Minnie was alive. But it would do nothing to appease her broken heart when she found out about Harris.

And then there was Mason's family.

Slowly, Spacey and part of the Louisville clan piled off the plane. The Louisville's were immediately shocked at how serene and luxurious the estate was. Mason had done his best to describe its magnificence but he definitely fell short.

By T. Styles

"This is beautiful," Shay said, stepping off the plane and walking behind Banks. "I wish Harris could've seen it."

Banks immediately turned around and gripped her by both arms forcefully. "Don't forget Minnie doesn't know yet." He whispered harshly, while looking back at Arlyndo and Howard who were carrying her off the aircraft. "So keep your fucking voice down."

"I'm sorry," she whispered. "But you shouldn't forget that I'm your daughter now too." She looked at his hands. "Would you be treating Minnie the way that you treating me now?"

He released her and took a deep breath. "Everybody follow me!" He yelled over her head.

When they got into the house, he paused when he smelled a familiar scent. He had been in the company of blood many times over his life, and knew something was up.

So did Mason.

"What the fuck happened here?" Mason said, breathing in the odor. He was limping a little but still ready to attack.

Banks looked back at him and then ahead. "I don't know."

After calling their names several times, Banks continued to move deeper into the house until he reached his bedroom. The beds were all made but no one was visible anywhere. Next he moved to Joey's room and still he found nothing or nobody. Finally he went to his staff members' house and they also were gone.

"I'll check the beach house," Mason said.

Banks nodded, forgetting momentarily that once again Mason knew the land because he'd been there without his knowledge.

After searching most of the property, finally Banks arrived at his lab. The closed door gave him pause but it didn't mean anything was out of the ordinary. Slowly he turned the knob, only to discover it was locked. Now he was concerned. Pretty sure that inside held the secrets to his questions, he jiggled the door harder and then..."Leave us alone!" Joey yelled.

"Joey, open the door!" Banks said banging on it with a closed fist.

"Pops?"

"Yeah, what's going on? Where is everybody?!"

The door unlocked and Joey yanked it open. Both him and Bet rushed up to Banks gripping him tightly, one on each side. "What happened?" Banks asked. "Where is the Nunez family?"

"I made a mistake," Bet cried looking up into his eyes. "I accidentally killed Oswalda."

"What?" Banks yelled. "Why?"

"POPS, WATCH OUT!" Joey yelled pointing at Mason who had hobbled up behind him. "MASON'S IN THE HOUSE! HE'S—"

"I know, son," he said calmly. "I flew them here."

"But I thought he was dead," Joey continued.

"Me too, it's a long story," Banks replied, still trying to wrap his mind around what he learned about Oswalda.

"Banks, you gotta come outside," Mason said hysterically.

"What now?"

"Somebody landing!"

"What?" He glared following him.

The entire family rushed outside, just to see a white plane land in front of the mansion on the landing strip, next to his aircraft. "Who is this?" Banks frowned at Mason. "You know 'bout this shit?"

"If I knew I wouldn't have needed the ride," he paused. "I put that on my kids."

When the door to the aircraft opened, the first person that stepped out jolted both of them.

It was Whoyawanmetabe.

Standing on the top step with a drink in hand, he smiled while overlooking the luxurious backdrop. "Hello, Wales' and Lou's! Glad ta see ya all t'gether again. 'Cause now we must tawk!"

COMING SOON

WAR 4:
SKULL ISLAND

CARTEL PUBLICATIONS

P R E S E N T S

The Cartel Publications Order Form

www.thecartelpublications.com

Inmates **ONLY** receive novels for $10.00 per book **PLUS** shipping fee **PER BOOK.**

(Mail Order **MUST** come from inmate directly to receive discount)

Shyt List 1	_____	$15.00
Shyt List 2	_____	$15.00
Shyt List 3	_____	$15.00
Shyt List 4	_____	$15.00
Shyt List 5	_____	$15.00
Pitbulls In A Skirt	_____	$15.00
Pitbulls In A Skirt 2	_____	$15.00
Pitbulls In A Skirt 3	_____	$15.00
Pitbulls In A Skirt 4	_____	$15.00
Pitbulls In A Skirt 5	_____	$15.00
Victoria's Secret	_____	$15.00
Poison 1	_____	$15.00
Poison 2	_____	$15.00
Hell Razor Honeys	_____	$15.00
Hell Razor Honeys 2	_____	$15.00
A Hustler's Son	_____	$15.00
A Hustler's Son 2	_____	$15.00
Black and Ugly	_____	$15.00
Black and Ugly As Ever	_____	$15.00
Ms Wayne & The Queens of DC **(LGBT)**	_____	$15.00
Black And The Ugliest	_____	$15.00
Year Of The Crackmom	_____	$15.00
Deadheads	_____	$15.00
The Face That Launched A Thousand Bullets	_____	$15.00
The Unusual Suspects	_____	$15.00
Paid In Blood	_____	$15.00
Raunchy	_____	$15.00
Raunchy 2	_____	$15.00
Raunchy 3	_____	$15.00
Mad Maxxx (4th Book Raunchy Series)	_____	$15.00
Quita's Dayscare Center	_____	$15.00
Quita's Dayscare Center 2	_____	$15.00
Pretty Kings	_____	$15.00
Pretty Kings 2	_____	$15.00
Pretty Kings 3	_____	$15.00
Pretty Kings 4	_____	$15.00
Silence Of The Nine	_____	$15.00
Silence Of The Nine 2	_____	$15.00
Silence Of The Nine 3	_____	$15.00
Prison Throne	_____	$15.00

By T. Styles

Drunk & Hot Girls	_____	$15.00
Hersband Material **(LGBT)**	_____	$15.00
The End: How To Write A	_____	$15.00
Bestselling Novel In 30 Days (Non-Fiction Guide)		
Upscale Kittens	_____	$15.00
Wake & Bake Boys	_____	$15.00
Young & Dumb	_____	$15.00
Young & Dumb 2: Vyce's Getback	_____	$15.00
Tranny 911 **(LGBT)**	_____	$15.00
Tranny 911: Dixie's Rise **(LGBT)**	_____	$15.00
First Comes Love, Then Comes Murder	_____	$15.00
Luxury Tax	_____	$15.00
The Lying King	_____	$15.00
Crazy Kind Of Love	_____	$15.00
Goon	_____	$15.00
And They Call Me God	_____	$15.00
The Ungrateful Bastards	_____	$15.00
Lipstick Dom **(LGBT)**	_____	$15.00
A School of Dolls **(LGBT)**	_____	$15.00
Hoetic Justice	_____	$15.00
KALI: Raunchy Relived	_____	$15.00
(5th Book in Raunchy Series)		
Skeezers	_____	$15.00
Skeezers 2	_____	$15.00
You Kissed Me, Now I Own You	_____	$15.00
Nefarious	_____	$15.00
Redbone 3: The Rise of The Fold	_____	$15.00
The Fold (4th Redbone Book)	_____	$15.00
Clown Niggas	_____	$15.00
The One You Shouldn't Trust	_____	$15.00
The WHORE The Wind		
Blew My Way	_____	$15.00
She Brings The Worst Kind	_____	$15.00
The House That Crack Built	_____	$15.00
The House That Crack Built 2	_____	$15.00
The House That Crack Built 3	_____	$15.00
The House That Crack Built 4	_____	$15.00
Level Up **(LGBT)**	_____	$15.00
Villains: It's Savage Season	_____	$15.00
Gay For My Bae	_____	$15.00
War	_____	$15.00
War 2: All Hell Breaks Loose	_____	$15.00
War 3: The Land Of The Lou's	_____	$15.00

(**Redbone 1 & 2** are **NOT** Cartel Publications novels and if **ordered** the cost is **FULL** price of $15.00 **each. No Exceptions**.)

Please add **$5.00** for shipping and handling fees for up to **(2) BOOKS PER ORDER**.

Inmates too!

The Cartel Publications * P.O. BOX 486 OWINGS MILLS MD 21117

(See Next Page for ORDER DETAILS)

Name: _____

Address: _____

City/State: _____

Contact/Email: _____

Please allow *8-10 __BUSINESS__* days __Before__ shipping.

The Cartel Publications is __NOT__ responsible for __Prison Orders__ rejected!

__NO RETURNS and NO REFUNDS__
__NO PERSONAL CHECKS ACCEPTED__
__STAMPS NO LONGER ACCEPTED__

By T. Styles